Isabelle's

Upstairs Coffee

Shop

By

Carmella Ann Schultes

This book is dedicated to my daughters and daughters

everywhere.

About the Author

Carmella is the mother of four daughters. She and her husband live in conservative, rural, northwest Iowa where they are openly liberal . It was a tumultuous election year and the opening of a private coffee shop that prompted her to write this piece of fiction. Members of the coffee shop inspired the characters in this story, however, Schultes utilized literary license in creating characters with traits not resembling the persons who inspired them.

Acknowledgements

I want to thank my husband, who never reads fiction, for offering to read my draft manuscript and for supporting, encouraging, and believing in me and my ability to write a book. I want to thank my friends Pat Spangler, Catherine Edgerton and Mike Rossman for also reading my manuscript and offering suggestions and guidance that hopefully helped me make it better. I want to thank the members of the real Upstairs Coffee Shop who in ways they may not even know, enriched my life and brought me joy. And always, I want to thank my daughters who because of their own work ethic and accomplishments inspire me every day to want to be purposeful and challenge myself.

TABLE OF CONTENTS

PART ONE

Chapter 1

Isabelle Potts pulled up to the curb in front of her studio and looked down the street as she turned off the car. It was cold and Main Street was deserted this early in the morning except for the two cars in front of the title company. Sitting at the end of the street stately and camouflaged by a gray sky behind it, the 200 year old Stone County Courthouse was nothing if not majestic for such a small hamlet as Lakeview. Isabelle never tired of the view and always gave a mental nod to the city fathers who had planned Lakeview and the placement of the courthouse in such a prominent location. It wasn't lost on her that the town had been settled by Germans whose influence and work ethic, though diluted over the generations, still defined the farming community in the rural communities of northwest Iowa. Nor was it lost on her that the descendents of those early immigrants were the very people who wanted to deport the modern day immigrant population. *"What had happened"*, she wondered. *"How could the spirit of adventure and fearlessness their forefathers had that drove them to cross an ocean and begin new lives have evolved in so few generation to a culture of fear, intolerance and nationalism that defined her friends and neighbors?"*

Isabelle opened her car door and stepped out onto the snow packed street grabbing her messenger bag and studio keys. It wasn't unusual for Isabelle to be the only one unlocking her business at 7:30 a.m.

most weekday mornings which meant she was always able to park in the same spot right in front of her studio door. In spite of the perfect parking spot, many was the morning Isabelle was tempted to park just two spots north for no other reason than to raise the ire of the nasty old lady who ran the office supply store next door to Isabelle's studio. More than once she had made it clear that she considered the spots in front of her door to be for her own customers and she had been so bold as to confront Isabelle on her right to leave her car there all day.

Though her frustrations with the community she felt so detached from on so many levels could make Isabelle pissy and retaliatory on an almost daily basis, for once Isabelle embraced her generous nature and played nice, parking a safe distance from the reserved spots.

Isabelle unlocked her door, ascended the 20 steps to

her upstairs studio, walked to the end of the 60 foot long narrow hallway leading to her office, hung her coat on the hall tree and pulled her lunch out of her messenger bag to put in the refrigerator.

Isabelle's studio was in suites five and six in a 187 year old building. The building had a lot of large windows which had been part of the appeal for the natural light they offered. The other suites on her floor were vacant.

Looking out her east windows was an alley where people that worked at the bank parked their cars. Looking north the view was of Stone County courthouse and the jail. To the south, Isabelle could look down on a crop of hollyhocks in June.But in the winter no matter which window she looked through, her best hope for seeing any color at all would be a car. And even that was not likely. Isabelle had noticed that conservative people in the country don't drive bright red, green or yellow cars. They drive white or taupe. (Isabelle's car was on the purple side of blue.) And they wear black or khaki coats.(Isabelle had a fuschia and an apple green coat.) And they keep their head down. It's safer that way, Isabelle guessed. So though her view lacked the colors one might see walking down a street of restored row houses in Washington DC, still, Isabelle loved her office suite in all the seasons, even winter. It had become her happy place.

Often Isabelle would fantasize about other uses for her leased space besides a photography studio. She would imagine it as a bookshop. It would have a piano in it and lots of comfy chairs. Sometimes she imagined it as a coffee shop with small intimate rooms and, because on both sides of her suite there were large windows on the other side of which were flat roofs covered in white waterproofing vinyl, she would imagine roof top patio seating. She had more than once been tempted to crawl out one of the north windows and sit on the roof of the office supply shop figuring if she didn't wear shoes and didn't walk around much she could get by w ith it. There she could pretend she was someplace else besides where she really was. But she always stopped short of crawling out the window because she feared the crabby lady whose roof she would be accused of violating.

Just north of Isabelle's studio on the street level and in the same block was a small clothing boutique run by a woman Isabelle's age, Carmen, and her daughter, Mary. Isabelle, had fallen in love with the clothing inventory they stocked resulting in her frequenting the boutique a few times a week. Isabelle came to rely on Carmen's and Mary's opinions when it came to her purchases and the threesome had developed a flourishing friendship so Isabelle not only had personal shoppers for her wardrobe but she had made new friends. Besides the boutique, for a while there had been a knit shop across the street. Isabelle had loved being able to go drink coffee (even though it was usually bad), knit with older ladies, hear the town gossip, and talk about everything she wished the town had. "Like a coffee shop," she would say to which everyone would agree. The knit shop owner was a smart, opinionated, strong and educated woman who had walked away from her Denver law practice seeking a meaningful life. Isabelle loved talking to her about life and politics. She had been absolutely refreshing offering Isabelle a new perspective on Lakeview and the idyllic life of the Lakevillians, for that was why she had left Denver. She had come looking for what Isabelle had had all along. And then one day her friend couldn't take paradise anymore so she left and moved to a larger city. Most days Isabelle would spend the entire morning working at her desk with no disruptions not even looking up until enough time had passed that she would discover it was almost noon.

 Isabelle sighed as she walked out of the kitchen with her coffee and walked to her office. Immediately Isabelle's mind turned to the tasks at hand for the day. She enjoyed a job with tons of flexibility and was able to structure her work day around her mood swings and her energy level. Most days she would spend the entire morning working at her desk with no disruptions not even looking up until enough time had passed that she would discover it was almost noon.

Isabelle sat down at her desk and opened her laptop to check her email. It was the first thing she did every morning after arriving at her studio and making herself a cup of coffee. With most of her work coming through email it was what would define her day. She had once been advised to never open email until she had first accomplished her list of tasks for the day but she just couldn't do it. The awareness that there was mail right at her fingertips and the temptation to find out what it contained was not something she could ignore. She had to know so she did what she always did and clicked her mail tab. The first message she opened shocked her and defined the rest of her day for sure and, as it would turn out, the rest of her year. This is what is said:

Hi Isabelle,

I wanted to let you know that starting this year we will be alternating prom photographers. Mary Phillips will be taking picures for us this year and if you are interested we would like you to take them next year. It is my understanding that a system

similar to this was followed in the past when staff

members were also photographers. I apologize for

the late notice but wanted you to know sooner than

later.

Hope Nelson, Lakeview High Staff

Isabelle read the message a second time and then sat

motionless staring out the window for the 15

seconds it took her to process what she had just

read. *I never really liked taking pictures anyway,"*

she thought as she pulled framed photos off the

walls. Photographing other people made her

nervous. She only did it because she needed

something more to do than just her job with the

Iowa Florist Association. And besides, one day the

florists would be ready for her to move on and what

could be better than to be a photographer who could

work when she wanted to, for whom she wanted, at

the price she wanted to. That was the plan when she opened, right?

And it really wasn't a bad plan six years ago when she started this chapter of her life. It was then when Ivy, the last of four daughters, was a senior in high school that Isabelle had opened her studio. Isabelle was aware that there was going to be a void in her life having spent most of the last 30 years focusing on her daughters only dabbling in photography, a little writing for the local paper, and volunteering for her church and the local school. The time seemed right to go real, instead of just being a hobby photographer. *"Why not open a studio and just make enough money to cover the $200 lease for the space?"* she had asked herself. By opening a studio she would also be able to do her work for the florists out of a real office in Lakeview, on main street, where she would not be as isolated as working from her home basement. Moving to a town office would open doors for more social engagement and maybe even becoming part of a community. And besides,the school had been contacting her for years to do their sports and groups photography when there was no other photo business in town. There was a window open she should jump through. And so she did. And that was that for 6 years. Until now.

But now that was about to be history too. Isabelle was making a decision that would change her course going forward and she couldn't help but think about what her husband Henry would say when she got home and told him she had closed her business today.

Henry hated to see Isabelle disappointed and would wrongly assume she was. She fully expected that when she told Henry, he would try to make her feel better and encourage her to keep the business open. But it wasn't going to work. This was her decision and Isabelle was tired. She was tired of dreading that someone would call and want to book a sitting. She was tired of dealing with people who were impossible to please like the mom who thought her senior son should not photograph as the redhead he was when she just saw him as having brown hair. She was tired of feeling guilty charging people for something she felt un-trained to do. She was tired of doing something that had always made her feel like a fraud. She wasn't tired of having her office in Lakeview and she had found some satisfaction in the social expansion of her life, but the photography business that had prompted the leasing of her upstairs office had not turned out to be that enjoyable.

At some point she had begun to see photography as

a potential profit opportunity really not expecting it would eventually make her feel like a fraud. And at first it didn't. Even after losing her school accounts, she would look at her own work more often than not concluding that it was good. In some cases very good. But that wasn't good enough on this day. Nothing she had done was good enough on this day. Right now she felt like a failure and a fraud and she wanted out.

Isabelle had actually been thinking recently of closing the studio and just doing off-site jobs. *"Or just passport pictures,"* she had thought. But not now. Not with this email. Things had just gotten easy for Isabelle. This was not a difficult decision for her. Having had her love of photography snuffed out by taking it too far, she had just been gifted the excuse she had been waiting for. And so she was jumping back through what she had thought was a window of opportunity and without doubting herself in the least she was going to close that window for good.

Isabelle finished taking down the gallery. She closed the facebook page, uninstalled her order program, packed up her equipment, and notified the Stone County Times to suspend her weekly ad. Busying herself all day with the un-doing of her business, she barely looked up until late afternoon when she went to the front door to peel her sign off. She stared through the glass door at Lakeview's main street. *"This was my business address,"* she thought. *"I've had a sign on this door for 6 years. But no more."* She was closed. There was still much to do, like selling her equipment and backgrounds, but she could deal with all of that later. Tomorrow she would rearrange her office suite and make it something new. For now she was just going to go home and break the news to Henry.

Isabelle made herself a cup of green tea for the road before she packed her messenger bag with her laptop, lunch boxes, and a book she was reading. Then she locked up her studio. As she got in her cold car Isabelle looked both ways down Main street to see if anything was going on. It wasn't much livelier than when she had last seen it that morning at 7:30. Across the street was a black guy walking south pushing a stroller which made Isabelle wonder how lonely and isolated he must feel in Lakeview where he had to know he wasn't welcome. There was no moving car in sight. *"If only just once in awhile I would have to wait for a car to pass by before I back up,"* Isabelle thought as she backed the car out and drove south toward the highway. Stopping at the corner, she smiled and waved at the black guy with the baby indicating he could cross and she would wait. She resisted the

temptation to lower her window and yell out, "I just

want you to know I think your life matters!"

Chapter 2

Isabelle wasn't really worried about announcing to Henry that she had closed her studio. Isabelle and Henry had first met when they were 7th graders. Isabelle was a town girl from a family of eight. Henry grew up on a farm. Henry claimed he had already been noticing Isabelle a few years before she fell in love with him in 9th grade. Throughout their decades of marriage he had made that claim never really convincing Isabelle it was true. But whatever the case for Henry, it wasn't until 9th grade that Isabelle noticed him. When Henry's mother died, Isabelle's empathy for Henry made her instantly fall in love with him and she knew right then that she wanted to take care of him for the rest of her life.

It took four years and a small team of her friends lobbying and encouraging him before Henry finally asked Isabelle on a date during their senior year. It would be years later that Henry would explain that he wanted to ask her out but he was afraid of her. Henry never dated anyone but Isabelle. He was smitten with her and years later Isabelle's mother would tell her that on being asked by one of their classmates how Henry and Isabelle were doing the classmate would comment "Henry was crazy about her".

Henry was of German ancestry which made him fit right into the community he had chosen to practice in. If you didn't know it from his surname, you would guess it from his work ethic. From the time he was old enough to reach the pedal on a tractor he was working alongside his dad on the farm or as a hired hand for a neighbor. Not a very big guy he was, nonetheless strong and stubborn, and the way he saw it, the true measure of a man was in his productivity and his integrity. So he was a good hire who always had work.

Throughout their marriage, Henry had done the heavy lifting when it came to providing income and financial security for their family and though Isabelle was proud of him she would lament that his German heritage was his worst enemy, or maybe hers. He simply did not know how to relax. He would work from dawn to dusk and when he wasn't working he was talking about working. And when he was talking about working he was talking about how to be more efficient and more productive.

If Henry and Isabelle were driving down the road, he would make out-loud observations about how someone needed to clean up around their acreage, or tear down an unused building. He would see dead trees that needed to be cut down and made into firewood, even if the owner didn't have a use for firewood. "You just don't waste stuff," he would say. If they went for a walk, Henry would notice a leaning retaining wall, a porch that was pulling away from the house, water pooling on sidewalks, peeling paint, crumbling steps, or expensive windows that didn't add anything to the house and made no sense. And he would always observe loudly, critically, and with an opinion presented as if it were fact. Yes, Henry was about as German as they come. And though Isabelle didn't really see that that was what she was signing up for when they married at 21 years of age, it didn't take long before she found out.

Isabelle would spend the rest of her married life adjusting to Henry's Germanness. She often thought, with some shame, that she and Henry just had different values. She liked to think that she valued experiences and time together over efficiency and productivity and she would be frustrated with Henry's long work days. But she shamed herself for such thoughts because she suspected it was only because of Henry's hard work and the security he provided that she could indulge her more idyllic value system.

Whatever their differences in that regard though, they were always pretty much aligned with each other on politics, religion, and frugality. Their closeness had only been reinforced by the political climate of Stone County. They both recognized how different they were from their conservative neighbors. Though Henry was better able to transcend it, they were both growing increasingly disenchanted with living in conservative rural Iowa.

The two of them had tag teamed the raising of four strong feminist daughters and were proud of that accomplishment. They were a pair, though they would often say "a pair of what?" to each other. But their teamwork along with humor, wit, and both being above average in intelligence had carried the day for over 40 years. And at the end of the day, though Isabelle especially would long for more social interaction and friendships, they were both happiest when they were together and alone. So life was good and marriage was great and they both knew they were very lucky indeed which is why Isabelle wasn't too worried about her news upsetting Henry.

In fact, Isabelle had been able to put it all out of her mind driving home that night and thinking about what tasks were waiting for her when she got there. There was always the drudgery of laundry. Then there was the mail, which was not the pleasure it was before she began her career in association management. Now days mail generally delivered work, not letters. Isabelle pulled the car into the detached garage, manually pulled down her remoteless garage door, and pulled her tiny watering-can key ring out of her bag to unlock the house deciding that summer couldn't come any too soon. The bitter north wind was getting old and she dreaded going out on the porch to gather wood to stoke up the living room fireplace.

As was her usual pattern she first lit a candle because she loved how the glow of a candle made everything warmer, then she walked around the house picking up … mostly her shoes and sweaters that somehow got strewn around the house making it appear that more than just two people lived in the monstrosity of a house. Before she knew it, the time had passed and she looked at her watch and saw that Henry should be home any minute.

Isabelle was pouring two glasses of wine as she always did for Henry and her to drink while they watched the 5:30 News Hour when she heard the basement door close signaling that Henry was upstairs.

"Hey, beautiful," Henry said as he always did when he came home from work. "How was your day?"

"Well," said Isabelle, "I closed the studio today".

"Really? Why did ya do that?"

Isabelle was not surprised when her husband didn't freak out about her knee jerk reaction after telling him about the email and her decision. Maybe he was finally used to her impulsiveness after 40 years. Maybe he had seen it coming. Or maybe he thought it was time, too. But he just assured her she was just up against odds that were out of her control.

"Not only are we not *native* Lakevillians," he said, "we aren't even contemporary Lakevillians. It makes a huge difference when you are trying to start a business here. You have been much more accepted than a lot of others might have been". Have been. There. Past tense. It was already history.

"Besides all that," Henry said, "you have to consider the economic depression of the county and the community, Isabelle. Over 50 percent of the kids in school are on free and reduced lunch. No one has the money for family portraits. You have to realize, Isabelle, we live in an area where people are poor. More than 14% of our population lives below the poverty line! We have a brain drain, here honey. Smart people move out for good jobs and what gets left behind are the uneducated, the disabled, the mentally challenged and a needy population."

Isabelle cringed at Henry's reference to the local economy fearing he would get on a rant about the entire world's economy that he loved to talk about. But to be fair, she too had long realized economic impacts on her business. Local economy aside, she had long known that with Facebook, affordable digital cameras, and smart phones, the professional photographer was another job being replaced by artificial intelligence. The market for selling pictures to families facing college tuition had already stagnated nationwide. There was an industry shift at work and had been for sometime. Senior pictures were going the way of the midcentury letter jacket.

Though the rural areas tended to resist progress, eventually they did follow suit. Many of Isabelles customers even though they were facing college tuitions weren't ready to give up the senior portrait tradition. For many of them high school graduation was a pinnacle milestone in their life but economic conditions had been forcing them to cut costs and it hadn't been hard for them to figure out that the cost to take 200 shots to get one good shot was all of $0.00 when you already had the camera. Photography was over and she and Henry both knew it. It was nice to have Henry recognize that and agree with her on something, for once.

They also both agreed that Isabelle had to keep her studio lease. The isolation of working from her home office was acceptable when there was a family to care for. Social exposure could be obtained at school events for the girls. But now with them grown and Henry at work all day, Isabelle had needed a place to work that got her out of the house.

That had really been the best outcome of the decision to open a studio back when she started her business.

"You have to continue to keep your studio, Isabelle," Henry said. "It makes you happy and it isn't like it's that expensive."

"I know," Isabelle said as she sorted the papers and magazines on the ottoman. "I will."

But as she went to the kitchen to make their supper, Isabelle's mind continued to circle around the issue rationalizing and justifying the idea. Though she hadn't really found her community per se in Lakeview, she had found a few new friends and she had been able to walk out her office and hop on her bike to go to the post office or the Family Dollar. Just those small changes to her life had made Isabelle measurably happier and a tiny bit less frustrated living in such a conservative alt right county. So even though the studio had actually made enough money to cover the lease, all of Henry and Isabelle's personal photo expenses, portraits for their daughter's family and more, the *real* benefit of the studio had been in its therapeutic value. Isabelle was happier working in town. She had never been a country girl, always preferring anonymity in a crowd over isolation in reclusiveness; she had grown up in a town and she liked working in town. Even Lakeview.

Standing in the kitchen later, Isabelle mindlessly chopped some onions and peppers to brown with some hamburger she was going to use to make chili for supper. It was a favorite of hers and she could do it from memory. She always made cornbread to go with it so mixing it up in her pre-occupied state of mind she continued to ruminate about not just the studio situation but their life more broadly. Isabelle opened a can of chili beans and tomato sauce and stirred them into the chili pot thinking about the path not taken. She recalled the day they drove to Lakeview the first time.

"We're getting close now," Henry had said. "That's it up ahead."

"Where? All I see is acres and acres of corn."

"Those elevators you see up ahead, " he had said. "That's the town."

It was Henry's job that had landed them here and at the time, with no awareness of it becoming permanent, Isabelle had been completely on board. It was new and they were young with two children. She was consumed with just being a good wife and mother. It would be years before she would grow restless with their rural life and long for something bigger and more vibrant. She wanted to walk to a coffee shop, a park with a walking trail, a used book shop and through neighborhoods of pretty houses. She hungered for diversity and multiculturalism. She ached for summer night strolls to park concerts, open air markets, and sidewalk restaurants. She had indeed come to regret their choice of 30 years ago but her main street studio actually had helped. Spending her days in Lakeview had been far more stimulating than being on their acreage alone everyday. Isabelle sighed audibly and called Henry in for supper.

It was too early to be eating supper on these short days with early night falls. Isabelle knew she was going to fall asleep on the sofa again before the Antiques Road Show was over which meant that about two a.m. she was going to be in the kitchen reading facebook and eating graham crackers and milk.

"Henry, we have to to start eating supper later!
Isabelle said as they sat eating.

Henry may have responded but all Isabelle
remembered the next morning was the slight
disturbance of Henry chewing his nightly cough
drop as she fell asleep after an exhausting day.

Chapter 3

It had to be the sound of the grinding coffee that woke Isabelle the next morning she was sleeping so deeply. Or maybe it was the smell of bacon or sautéing garlic. It was still dark and the temperature in the room was only 60 degrees. Isabelle pulled the covers around her and burrowed down while she waited for Henry to come back to bed with their morning coffee. It was the way they started every day. Henry would hear the dog scratching at the door which was his cue to get up and go downstairs to start the coffee, let the dog out, and turn the heat up. He would putter around while their espresso machine warmed up, feeding the dog, filling his water bowl, starting some breakfast and then return with the coffee, having let Isabelle sleep another 15 minutes while the furnace ran and warmed up the room.

The old drafty arts-and-crafts style home had been a wonderful place to raise a family. It was Henry who saw the potential for the house when they had purchased it in 1983 during the farm crisis. It was a foreclosure that had sat empty for a year. Isabelle remembered the first morning she had woken up in the house. They had worked on it for 6 months before moving in December 6 that year, determined to start building memories by being moved before Christmas. Isabelle remembered coming down the stairs looking at her large kitchen with the beautiful oak cabinetry and the south facing windows that first morning. The light had streamed in capturing the dancing dust particles as it warmed the kitchen with a magical glow. Her little girls had all still been asleep wrapped in the quiet of the house that first morning as Isabelle had stood on the kitchen step to the landing and looked at her new home hardly believing it was true. The house was ready for her family. The stories yet to be written and memories yet to be made had a home and could begin to unfold. The very step Isabelle had been standing on would later come to be known as the naughty step where her toddlers would sit for 5 minutes to ponder their behavior. But on that morning such a memory remained yet unknown and it had been enough for Isabelle's soul to be filled with just the light from the windows and the quiet of the family slumbering in their beds. She could wait a lifetime to be warmed by memories.

They had worked so hard those six months. Isabelle had had her daughter Sammy right about the time they bought the house and, like her older sister

Andy, Sammy had been a colicky baby. With so much work to do before they moved in, Isabelle and Henry had set up a crib and spent every evening at the house trying to get it ready for their family's habitation. Isabelle remembered the frustration many of those nights walking the floor with Sammy, seeing so much work that needed to be done and not being able to do any of it. Their friends had helped. And on moving day their friends are who got them and their three little girls quickly moved in in just one day.

Often when Isabelle was distraught over living in Stone County surrounded by home schoolers, Christian fundamentalists, and gun rights advocates, she would remember that move and those people. The move from their rental had been only seven miles but for Henry and Isabelle with his job, their two small children and a newborn it might as well have been across the state. Isabelle had been packing and marking boxes for weeks while Henry was at work. Everyone in town had heard they were moving.

Since arriving in the community, they had been living in a fishbowl with the ups and downs that come with living so transparently in a small community. They would be finding out soon one of the ups. Over the course of those weeks whenever a client had offered to help with the move, Henry had just responded that it would help if they could stop by with their pickup and haul a load for him. The day they moved Isabelle stayed at their rental to push boxes to movers and Henry stayed at the new house where loaded trucks just kept showing up. Isabelle would look out the window and there would be three trucks in her driveway in line ready to pick up boxes. She would direct them to a pile and off they would go to empty their truck at the new house before going on about their day. Only a few trucks would make back and forth trips sticking with the move until it was done. It had been unbelievable to Isabelle that so many people had come to help them.

Henry and Isabelle had gone to sleep that first night with most of the house in a state of order and, in Isabelle's memory, almost every box unpacked. It had been exhausting and emotional and they couldn't have done it without so many kind people helping them, the same people who were now these 30 years later putting her county in the national spotlight for their alt right political positions.

One of Isabelle's most vivid memories of their move was walking through the kitchen after the last box from their rental had been loaded and she had finally arrived at the new house and seeing someone cleaning her oven and stove so that it would be like a new brand new stove in their brand new house. Over the years they would come to take for granted what they had, but every now and then they would have a guest remind them how lucky they were to have a home of such stature and craftsmanship and they would admonish themselves for taking for granted their good fortune. And they would remember that moving day and be humbled by the kindness of the community in coming to help them. Recently Isabelle would ask herself, "What happened? When did I lose that feeling about my community? Have I changed? Have they changed?" What she was pretty sure of was that had she and Henry been black and not the new veterinarian in town, they would most likely have been moving alone.

In spite of warm sunny glows, cherished memories,

and architectural integrity, a 1917 house is cold. The walls of houses built in 1917 had poor insulation if they had any at all. And, unless major expense had been incurred by someone to remedy that, it was as true now as it was 30 years ago. In January when it is so terribly cold outside, frost collects on the inside of the upstairs bedroom windows where it is not even possible to keep the temperature at 70 degrees. Though they had often referred to themselves as the Waltons, Isabelle and Henry had done alright. In fact they were reminded of it every morning when Henry made their coffee using their Gaggia grinder and pulling their espresso shots from their La Pavoni espresso machine. Then while sipping their Americanas in bed they convinced each other that they were probably drinking the best coffee in the world, or at least the county, to start their day.

Usually it took long enough to drink their coffee that the furnace had kicked in and the bathroom had warmed by the time Isabelle was dashing across the hall with her arms full of the clothes she had picked out for the day. By then the bathroom would be feeling like a sauna which was just the way she liked it.

Though Isabelle could have worn anything she wanted to work, since she rarely saw anyone, she spent time every morning *carefully choosing* what she wore. It wasn't as if anyone even came to her office. At most she might skype someone who would see her so it really wouldn't even have mattered if she had stayed in her pajamas all day long, on the days she worked from home. But Isabelle preferred not to work from home most days and she cared how she looked to herself everyday, so Isabelle would pull out two or three options every morning before she would make a decision and even then she sometimes changed three times before she left the house. She had once heard a teacher acquaintance say that she selected her outfits for the entire week every Sunday night claiming it made for efficiency in morning routines. Isabelle didn't understand why anyone had to be that efficient unless they were German like Henry. Isabelle had to dress for her mood and she liked choosing her clothes every morning. So that is what she did.

On this day, Isabelle knew she was going to be moving furniture, making trips to the thrift store and recycling so she chose some skinny jeans that would tuck in her sorrels and an orange wool sweater she had knit last winter. She would almost always finish off the outfit with a scarf to contrast or brighten the ensemble sometimes commenting "I feel edgy today, Henry. Does this look edgy?" to which Henry would comment "Just express it in your clothes Isabelle and be nice." With the orange sweater she paired a red floral scarf that would defy convention and she was set for the day! Once dressed, just before she left the bedroom Isabelle would give herself a good spritz of Tova. Then she would head downstairs to the good sounds and smells sizzling away on the stove where Henry would be cooking their breakfast.

Henry would normally be in the kitchen sauteing garlic for scrambled eggs before Isabelle would have her wardrobe figured out and today was no different. While Henry made breakfast every morning Isabelle would pack their lunch which they would eat in the studio kitchen just like they had almost every day for the last six years. Isabelle really could have eaten out every day but there was no place in Lakeview where a healthy lunch could be purchased. So she would stuff some olives, peppers, bacon bits, and cranberries in a mason jar, pour in her homemade vinaigrette and then stuff in some lettuce. Voila … salad in a jar and lunch was ready to go. It was their routine. And Henry, especially, was very much a routine person. In fact Isabelle often thought he was in a rut he was so routine. But *she*, decisively, was *not* in a rut. And yesterday was proof of that if proof were needed, Isabelle thought. *"Today I begin life without a photography business"*. Which made her eager to get to the studio and begin to re-invent her space.

Chapter 4

Isabelle was lucky that her paid job was so flexible. So on a day like today when she had a project that was obsessing her, she could manage to work around it. Isabelle was at her office before eight a.m. After unlocking the door and ascending the long staircase, she pondered what to tackle first. "*It makes sense to discard first*," Isabelle thought.

Isabelle's suite had once been an apartment so she had a very small kitchen with an apartment sized stove where she would brew her espresso in a stove-top moka pot. Isabelle made herself a cup of coffee and then took it into what had been the green dressing room to begin. She sat down in the maroon wing back chair she had managed to fit into the small room that overlooked the alley. She remembered her son in law helping her hang the bamboo shades and twin vertical mirrors and her daughter May and her painting the walls pea green, a color she was still fond of. On one wall was a dresser and mirror where she had stored props and necessities for her customers and that was where she would start.

Opening the drawers Isabelle was surprised to discover how much she had accumulated in just six short years. Isabelle had always tried to be mindful of how much work it would be to move *out* of the studio, so she thought she had been sparing about what she had moved *into* the studio. But walking around the dressing room there was no denying how much "stuff" she had accumulated and how much purging she was going to have to do. She started tossing into the trash bin all the makeup items she had kept on hand for senior girls. She allowed herself one drawer to keep things in that she might use after which she started to make a pile for the thrift store. She had kept sheets and a blow up at the studio in case she and Henry had ever had to stay over because of a blizzard. There was the cheap iron and table-top ironing board that had been available in case a senior boy had pulled out a crumpled dress shirt not fit to be photographed in. Into the thrift store pile she tossed curling irons, a hairdryer, colored boas, hats, small props for babies, baby headbands, baby girl tutus, and toys. Isabelle boxed everything up and then two hours later trekked down the sidewalk carrying the box to the thrift store where she knew they took everything. *"In fact some of this stuff probably came from there."* she thought as she headed back.

Isabelle stood in the middle of the former consultation room and looked into the, now empty, former dressing room. She thought about where she would like her desk. Deciding it would be nice to finally have her desk in the consultation room that has a view of the hallway and a south facing window she proceeded to disassemble all of her electronics and desk contents to make May's antique teacher's desk light enough that she could shove it through the doorway. She also had to disassemble her large library table that had been her consultation table. It would be hauled home, but she knew she would have to get Henry to help with that. She had been known to move refrigerators and pianos around between rooms but hauling that heavy table down the long flight of stairs was a different issue. She could see herself losing control and watching her table crash through the glass door onto the sidewalk on Mainstreet. *"Lordy,"* Isabelle thought to herself, *"As if I need one more reason for people to think I'm strange!"*

The disassembly of the desk and the table reminded Isabelle of how frugal she and Henry had been over the years scrounging to furnish their house with strong solid pieces. The desk was a massive oak teacher's desk with a file drawer and two pull out writing boards. Henry had been offered it by a client one time when he had their little seven year old May with him on a call. The farmer had managed to get the shy little thing to talk to him when he found out she liked to play school. He had said, "I just might have something for you if your dad will let you have it!" That day a very happy seven year old came home with a desk tied to the top of the vet truck that had drawers that were as heavy as she was. Over the years that desk had been put to use in various places around the house and then the studio, someday to be claimed by its rightful owner and be hauled away.

Like that desk the large library table Isabelle broke down to take back home had its story. *"Most tables do,"* Isabelle thought. In fact, Isabelle believed that tables were the single most important piece of furniture in a home because it was around the table where families interacted. Tables, especially kitchen tables, were where decisions were made, games were played, meals were shared, letters were written, homework was done and so much more. She found herself never able to discard any table she ever had and always wondering about the stories that went with every old table she ever saw. This old table had been a jumble store find when the girls were very small and they had moved into their big house. Henry had hauled it home, taken it apart, sanded, stripped, refinished and re-glued it. It had served the family well for many years and Isabelle loved it.

Isabelle worked all afternoon moving, sorting, tossing, re-organizing drawers and by noon she had a new office. She was pleased. It was a larger office in its new room that also offered a great view down the long hallway. One of the best changes to her space was that the old smaller office which had been in the red room had been converted to a coffee lounge where she had placed a small drug store table and four chairs her dad had saved for her from a drug store he had purchased in 1960. It would be where she and Henry could have lunch or she and friends could have coffee. The old dressing room now held the comfortable wing back chairs and a cube where she could relax with a book. The whole suite of rooms was very cozy and inviting, especially after she added a small electric fireplace and a few candles. *"Yes,"* thought Isabelle. *"This will do quite nicely. This will do for a few more years and I'll figure out something else to do instead of photography. Maybe I'll become an activist!"* she thought.

Chapter 5

It was an election year and since her girls were raised, Isabelle had become very interested in politics. In fact she had been engaged since early fall in helping with the Hillary campaign that had taken up much of her time. She had hosted house parties, door knocked, attended meetings and phone webinars as well as phone banked. It was really not her style to be so public with her politics and she was growing less enthused about the grassroots work the longer she helped, but she was at the same time becoming increasingly enraged at the way women were still being treated, so bailing was not a choice. She had had enough of good old boy politics and she was going to see this through!

Isabelle had long believed it was time for a woman to be president and she had committed to doing her part to make that happen. And if it didn't happen she would at least be able to live with herself for having not sat by and done nothing. So she had already made the campaign to elect Hillary Clinton her public service project for the year. Why not go full throttle and challenge Stone County's political status quo? Isabelle envisioned using her re-purposed office space for meeting up with other lonely progressives who might be interested in political activism ... if she could find them. *"There must be others out there in the shadows of Stone County",* she thought.

Luckily, Isabelle had found one person already who was equally if not more passionate about Hillary than she was. And together she and her friend Clarys had formed a pact to stay in for the long haul.

Isabelle and Clarys were a bit like a couple of school girl besties. They had made their pledges that this was what they were going to do and they were not going to let each other down. They were a team and they would work as a team. And that was that, even though they both felt like the lonely Maytag repairman supporting a locally unpopular candidate for the locally unpopular party.

Isabelle and Clarys had actually known each other for over a decade. In fact they shared fond memories of getting together for tea when their oldest daughters were in middle school. But as so often happens with friendships formed because of children, friendships can end because of children. And that is exactly what had happened. It hadn't helped that they lived in different towns. But probably due more to their daughter's friendship not surviving middle school, than to anything else, Isabelle and Clarys had allowed their friendship to fizzle out. For over ten years, whenever they saw each other they would both express genuine delight immediately followed by awkward silence for lack of having anything to say to each other.

When Isabelle started working in Lakeview, she had tried to revive her friendship with Clarys. Many things had changed and since she had always regretted their unrealized friendship she would have welcomed reconnecting. Running into each other twice over the last six years since she had opened her studio, they had stopped and chatted on the sidewalk. "We should get together," Isabelle would suggest to which Clarys would agree. Then they would share an email address or their phone numbers and promise to set something up after which Isabelle would wait to hear from Clarys and nothing would happen. Eventually, Isabelle decided she was pushing a friendship that only she wanted or cared about so she gave up. And then, unexpectedly, over politics of all things, their paths crossed again.

Isabelle and Clarys were quite different from each other in many ways. Isabelle was structured, organized, and focused. Clarys was random and generally out of control of her life. Probably because of their differences, Isabelle saw Clarys as a free spirit with a kind heart who would make Isabelle a better person just by spending time with her. Clarys saw Isabelle as a smart, take charge person who had her act together, an influence she could benefit from. They were both a little right. They were both a little wrong.

Clarys had been dropping into the studio on occasion since their friendship had been renewed and just as Isabelle was sitting down in her new office one morning, she heard the front door close and Clary's heavy footsteps ascending the stairs.

"What the heck are you doing?" Clarys asked when she walked into the new office where Isabelle had moved her desk.

"I closed the studio."

"No! Please don't tell me you're leaving Lakeshore. I might have to shoot myself!" Clarys had found more than friendship in Isabelle. Isabelle had become her life coach of late.

"No worries, Clarys. I can't give up my office. I just needed a new look and a new purpose. I'm not going anywhere," Isabelle said.

"But what happened? Why did you close the studio?'

As Isabelle explained the loss of the school's prom shooting and her reliance on the school for her profit margin she shared how she got into photography in the first place.

"I bought my first camera the first year Henry and I were married. I actually bought it for Henry but I used it more than he did. When we were in college we would go walking around neighborhoods and take pictures of our favorite houses so that someday when we were *really* grown up and could afford it, we would use the pictures to show the builder what we wanted."

"Do you still have them?"

"Oh, heavens no! One time I purged a bunch of negatives and I'm sure they are long gone! Anyway, when Henry was in veterinary school and I was teaching high school, my passion for photography spilled over into my teaching. I inspired students to love photography. I was the yearbook instructor in this little tiny rural school and the kids there had no aspirations other than to become 'sod busters' like their dads. I had secured a couple of 35 mm cameras from the company that printed our yearbooks so I made a presentation to the school board and got them to approve my purchasing equipment for a dark room. See, I was the librarian and I had this little media room with a sink I wasn't using and I could see it as being just perfect. It was right in the library where my desk was and I could keep an eye on it."

"Wait … you used to be a librarian?" Clarys asked.

"Just for a short time while I taught a few English classes, but yes. Anyway, it was a proud day for me when three of my senior boys got cameras for their graduation gifts the last year I was there. I felt like I had really touched those students and launched them on a path that might be a lifelong hobby."

"So where did you learn how to take pictures?"

"As the girls started coming, I wanted to document their growth with portraits but we really couldn't afford that. So I would do photo shoots of them myself. What I saved in sitting fees at professional studios eventually funded more lenses, flashes, plenty of film, and enlarging anything I wanted. Next thing I knew friends would ask me to take pictures for them or sometimes I would ask if I could shoot them just for practice and for fun. Anyway one thing led to another and I was shooting for pay. I never started out with that intention." Isabelle finished.

"Oh, it makes me sad that you closed your studio."

"Well," said Isabelle, "get over it because we have a

new project. You are about to become a local

political activist, Clarys. We'll see how things go,

but you might be sitting in the Stone County

Progressives Situation Room, right now! We are

coming out of the shadows."

Chapter 6

Over the next few weeks there was limited if any
political strategizing but the seed had been planted
and that was enough for now. Meanwhile, Isabelle
was loving going to her office every day where
opening her mail and taking care of the work for the
florists from her new workplace made work more
fun. On days when her work was caught up by
early afternoon, she would often take her knitting or
a book into her sitting room spending the entire
afternoon sitting by her cozy fireplace sipping tea or
espresso that she had made in her stove-top moka
pot. She read until late afternoon when she would
gather her things and head home to start her usual
routine. She was patiently waiting for something to
trigger her newly identified purpose. There really

was nothing left to do to close out her photography business other than do something with their beloved library table that had been moved out of the studio only to be dumped in the entry way at home where it still sat.

Although they had talked about where to put it, Isabelle and Henry had not been able to decide. "I love this table," Isabelle said. "I really don't want to put it in the attic. It just makes no sense to haul something up to the attic. You have to ask yourself, 'Why am I hauling this up here? For what purpose?" she said. Henry agreed but pointed out that the basement was not a good place. Both of them were thinking they wished there was just someplace they could use it in their house even though they knew their house was already full of furniture. So uncharacteristically for them, they had procrastinated moving the table out of the entry way where it had remained for the past two weeks.

During the 30 years since they had purchased the table at an antique store they had grown attached to it. Isabelle had memories of mixing cakes, cookies and breads, rolling out cinnamon rolls, and patting out biscuits on this table. Hundreds of jars of canned beans, beets, and tomatoes had been filled with four sets of little hands from their four little girls standing around it, standing in chairs when they were little but not wanting to be left out, reaching their little pudgy hands into the bowls of snap peas or beans to fill freezer bags or push vegetables into jars through the the canning funnel. Their little girls had colored countless pictures, died dozens of Easter eggs, pressed lots of pansies and made hundreds of playdoh characters. Friends and family had drank many cups of coffee while sitting around it and Isabelle had served countless meals to her young growing family before they had finally outgrown it and moved to a proper dining table and chairs.

The library table had been perfect while they had used it. Ingrained in its patina were little scratches and chips and rings from wet glasses … visible memories of a family now grown and separated. It was a tangible piece of their past that kept Henry and Isabelle from wanting to part with it. As their daughters had grown older and married many political discussions were held around the kitchen table in their home, but that all came after their library table had been retired. Social activism, political engagement, discussions about local politics were not part of the story of the library table as they knew it. Not yet.

On one of the long sides of the table were two shallow but deep drawers where napkins had been stored. If you were sitting on that side of the table and someone needed a napkin you had to lean back and pull the drawer against your chest to fish one out for them. It was one of the annoying inconveniences that made it memorable long after it was no longer useful. Years later, Ivy, the youngest of her children told Isabelle that she always wanted to sit on the side with drawers having loved getting napkins out when someone needed one because it had always made her feel useful to the family when she had a job no one else could do. It was a solid table with no expansion potential and because of that no cracks going across it to imbalance a glass of milk or through which spilled milk could run onto the floor or one's lap.

It was a table like no other not really having been built for the way they had used it which is also why it had outlived its usefulness for them, or so they thought. Henry and Isabelle were not used to leaving things undone. But that table had been sitting in the way for too long now. "Well let's figure it out and get it out of here this weekend," Isabelle said as she was leaving for the office one morning. "It's in the way and I want to get it moved somewhere." And with that she had headed out the door to go to work while Henry left by way of the basement stairs to head off to work himself.

The roads were slick again that morning driving to her office. Isabelle didn't drive over 45 miles per hour into the winds that had grown increasingly forceful since the day before. Isabelle had heard it howling throughout the night and with a blizzard forecast she was not surprised to see dark foreboding clouds as she turned west toward Lakeview. The sky was a midnight blue almost fading to black in the northwest direction from which their winter weather came.

Isabelle was glad she had layered her outfit, wearing leggings under her skinny jeans with her favorite light weight cami under a favorite wool sweater which she had layered over a long sleeve shirt. Around her neck she wore a gray scarf she had received for Christmas from her daughter May that was knit from Chilean alpaca. Above her Sorel boots, that were exactly like her daughter Andy's, peeked her lavender leg warmers that Ivy had knit Isabelle from mohair for her birthday last year. And lastly she wore a long hand-me-down down coat from Sammy and her stocking cap from the sale rack at Cabela's. Isabelle mused that morning that she was taking literally the expression that she was wearing her heart on her sleeve; her girls were all over her!

Isabelle always wore a hat in the winter and didn't

understand why everyone didn't. She suspected

most people didn't want to smash their hair but that

wasn't an issue with Isabelle. She wore her thick

gray hair long and either in a braid or a bun or just

flowing. She fully knew that there were those who

thought women her age shouldn't wear long hair.

And many was the time she had heard her own

mother comment about some hillbilly in long

straggly hair. But Isabelle knew she had beautiful

hair and with her full set of teeth to go with it, she

figured she could pass for civil with a touch of

individualism. *"To each his own,"* she thought.

Today she was wearing orange and lilac and gray.

"Intentionally and tastefully un-coordinated,"

Isabelle thought.

Isabelle had always tried to define herself outside

the confines and the context of her geographic

existence. Not only did she resist dressing like

everyone else in Lakeview and nearby Lakeshore but she liked to do her own thinking. Some years ago she had let her daughter Sammy paint favorite quotes on a few walls in the house and she had been very tempted to have her paint something she remembered her dad always saying. Raising his family in the 60's and 70's, it had to have been a frightening time to be a parent. The Vietnam war, the civil unrest brought on by the civil rights movement, the culture of free love and free drugs, the feminist movement … those were all huge influences on the culture and the young people growing up at the time. Isabelle's dad had always said to his kids to do their own thinking.

Isabelle doubted that her dad had been a praying man. He wasn't a religious man so he must have resorted to counting on his kids taking his advice and making smart decisions. It had worked. All of his kids had survived the 60's and 70's with no drugs, no pregnancies, and no arrests. By the time most of his kids had aligned themselves with the side of racial tolerance and inclusion and two of his three daughters had become self proclaimed feminists, her father had passed on but his advice was something Isabelle had carried with her her entire life and she believed it was one of the best gifts he had given her. Her father had not only given her that advice, but intended or not, he had given her permission to be a feminist woman who could and should do her own thinking and she had taken it to heart and been empowered by it. It didn't bother her that she might have been seen by others as a little strange and non-conforming. She could only imagine that were her name to even come up in conversation among women in rural Lakeview there would be a few eye rolls. Her style was individual and unconventional in every way; from how she parented to how she dressed.

It didn't go unnoticed that Isabelle liked to shake things up a bit. Like the time she headed up the bible school program and flipped it from mornings to evenings, recruited the church ladies to provide a meal for the volunteer parents who had worked all day, and engaged more men in the hands on activities with the children. *"Men helping with bible school? That was a novel idea! Isn't that women's work?"* Isabelle suffered no fools. She had long since given up on being popular and had decided that the cost of that was too dear. She wanted to be the example to her daughters of the kind of women she wanted them to become and she recognized that to do that in Lakeview was going to take social courage and independent thinking on her part. Sometimes the pathway to success was not the path of least resistance. Isabelle had a "bring it on" attitude.

 Not so much when it came to inclement weather, though! Before driving to the office on slick roads that morning, Isabelle had checked weather reports and according to the internet it was colder in Lakeview than it was in Moscow, Anchorage, Minneapolis, Chicago and of course Kansas City. Isabelle checked every day. In her mind, if she was going to endure this arctic tundra of a pathetic existence, by god she was going to have bragging rights.

She had all the cities where her daughters and siblings lived saved on her phone and she checked every day to see who had it the worst. Though she would have never admitted having any of her Southern Missouri mother's personality, she would joke that she sure knew what suffer'n was and keeping those city temps at the ready was her proof to herself that no one was suffer'n more than she was! Isabelle liked to mention to Henry, whom she shamefully blamed for landing them in Stone County, that they were colder than anyplace else in the world that day. The days could be endlessly dreary with no sun for weeks in January and February and Isabelle longed for just a change of scenery some days. Her thoughts always returned to how she would have loved a coffee shop to escape to. In fact she once drove 40 miles just to work in one from her laptop and then drove home again two hours and a few cups of coffee later.

"JEEPERS, its cold!" Isabelle said to herself as she shivered and crept slowly down the highway. "I sooo need a vacation somewhere warm and cheery!" But vacation was not in the cards for Isabelle any time soon. The Iowa caucuses were in

February and she had work to do. No matter how cold it was.

Chapter 7

With the Iowa Caucuses looming Clarys and Isabelle had been hitting the door-knocking pretty hard. They had lists of addresses they were to visit and re-visit and then the last weekend before the caucuses they were supposed to do a final visit to all the same addresses again. Grumbling about the ridiculousness of that strategy for a town like Lakeview, Isabelle and Clarys nonetheless had made the commitment and they were true to their word. They would always meet upstairs in Isabelle's office for coffee before they descended the long stairway to Isabelle's car. Isabelle always drove which worked just great for them both. Isabelle was a terrible passenger and Clarys was a great passenger except for Isabelle always having to make Clarys put on her seat belt. *"It's as if she doesn't hear the car dinging at her,"* Isabelle thought. Eventually Clarys would buckle up and then they would drive around pulling up to crumbling curbs, starting and stopping on each block to get out, and sliding and slipping down sidewalks packed with ice where there were sidewalks, trudging through snow where residents hadn't shoveled the walk clean, and knocking on doors. They spent most of the last two weeks of January doing their civic and political duty and being very glad when they could check off all the names on a page of addresses. They both agreed that neither of them would have done it if it were not for the other and then near the end of the two weeks and still not quite through every page of addresses, they learned that both of them had travel plans that was going to require they split up and work alone in order to finish out the lists by the deadline they had been given. To make it worse they were being given another town.

Isabelle didn't actually live in Lakeview. Her residential address for the last 30 years had been in the much smaller much more depressing sister city of Lakeshore where they were now expected to door knock. Lakeview might be where Isabelle worked and where she identified but she had to list Lakeshore as the address where she lived. Lakeshore was so not important in the campaign that it hadn't even been on the campaign's radar until the last few weeks when the field representatives saw that there was time to knock more doors and decided to assign them to Clarys and Isabelle.

Isabelle had often referred to Lakeshore as the armpit of the county, which though seemingly unkind and very unflattering was actually not so far off the mark. Lakeshore was always in the paper it seemed for drug busts, domestic disputes, and petty crimes. It was a town that had lost everything including its churches, schools, retail businesses, newspaper, gas stations, a car dealership and more. Isabelle and Henry had been there to see much of the decline in the 80's and it hadn't been pretty. It wasn't hard to recognize that it was Lakeshore that made Stone County's rankings for percent of people living below the poverty line so high. Little towns like Lakeshore were where the poorest of the poor were living.

The farm crisis that had led to a massive exodus of the population had in doing so caused the downward spiral that led to the many closures and now after a few decades of economic depression it was showing up in the deteriorating houses and crumbling infrastructure and in the paper in

reported drug busts and domestic assaults. The

people who had been left behind after the exodus of

the 80's were older, disabled, uneducated, and often

struggling with dependencies or mental health

diseases. The toll on the town had been marked.

There were those who had refused to accept the

death of their community and they would rally at

times. Like when it was time for the annual summer

parade. Or when the city got a grant for a

community center and library. Or when they started

a weekly farmers market., which turned out to be a

sad gathering of older people hungry for some

social engagement and a few people buying the

produce.

Not much Lakeshore had tried ever worked. The

parade had fewer and fewer spectators every year.

Eventually the architect of the market idea couldn't

take living there anymore giving up and moving away herself leaving the market to die without her there to run it. The new library/community center funded with a government grant, a concept lost on the residents who hated big government, became a refuge where poor kids would go to play games on the computer and locals would go to find Christian fiction and Hallmark and Veggie Tales movies.

 Isabelle hated going to Lakeshore. The houses where the poorest were living should have been condemned which depressed her. The dogs that ran loose and were commonly pit bulls or pit bull crosses terrified her and the ones that were neglected tied up living on a dirt patch saddened her Nonetheless, Isabelle offered to door knock Lakeshore by herself since Clarys would be covering the last weekend in Lakeview by herself.

So on a Monday afternoon, knowing she could

canvas the entire town in a few hours, Isabelle found herself setting out with her list of addresses and brochures in hand. And it was then, when she was looking at her list, that she began to wonder what she had gotten herself into. She knew these people! And if there is one thing people don't talk about in small towns it's politics. Because if you talk about politics you might offend someone you care about. And now here she was going up to houses, uninvited, knocking on doors possibly during someone's nap or favorite game show to talk about politics, Isabelle was regretting that she had offered to walk Lakeshore alone or even at all.

It wasn't that she cared what anyone thought really, but she did care about many of the people. These were people she had sat by in church. They had babysat for her, taught her little girls in Sunday School. They might have driven her girls' school bus or cheered them at little league ball games. There were memories of little Sammy always knowing John would get candy out of his pocket during church and pass it over the pew to her if she was good. And Andy and May had memories of walking down the church aisle many Sunday's with Old Joe, the elder in charge of candles and offering who had to be older than God and who wore the same suit and cowboy boots every week. Andy and May would giggle sitting by Joe in the back of the church listening to his soft snoring giving him an elbow when the organist cut loose on "Praise God From Whom All Blessings Flow". All the way home they would talk about his snoring and the hair growing out his ears convincing little Ivy it was long enough to comb. The whole Potts family had a soft spot for Joe and John and a lot of other people in Lakeshore.

Isabelle may not really want to identify with the town, she flippantly referred to it as the armpit of the state, but Isabelle always knew that many of the people she cared about and who had cared about her did still live there and they loved their town. Yes, they were the people who proudly flew their American flags and robustly advocated for their second amendment rights. They were God fearing fundamentalists hating big government and fearing change. But ... there was good in these people. Isabelle knew it. She had seen it.

And now here she was approaching them uninvited to peddle her liberal feminist politics. Realistically she doubted she was doing the campaign any real good anyway in a town where she was known to be a little on the wack-a-doodle side of normal. Missing the company of Clarys, Isabelle decided that door-knocking was one of those things that is a lot more fun to do with someone else.

Luckily there were few people home in the middle of a work day. Or at least few people who answered to her gentle knock, which was followed by a quick retreat. Knocking doors at vacated houses helped to make the afternoon fly by for the most part. Besides there being few people at home to answer the door there were several people on the list she could skip because Isabelle knew she could do more harm than good if they knew who she was supporting. *"You sometimes just have a feel for that sort of thing,"* Isabelle thought, *"so you make an executive decision about those contacts. You skip them, move on down the sidewalk, and go ahead and mark them as not home."* And that was just what she did.

By three o'clock that afternoon, feeling grateful there were just a few doors left to knock Isabelle teetered precariously along the icy sidewalk to the last house on Elm street occupied by someone whose name she didn't recognize. Carefully climbing the cracked, crumbling and sloping steps packed in ice and snow, Isabelle knocked gently on the storm door that wouldn't quite close all the way. And then, ever so quietly, just as she had been doing for the last hour, Isabelle made a hasty retreat hoping no one had time to answer the door before she would already be gone. Finding herself halfway down the sidewalk before Isabelle heard someone call, "Can I help you?" she turned around to see a young woman leaning out the door with a phone to her ear, Isabelle groaned internally and waved dismissively and said "Oh, I'm just a local volunteer with the Hillary campaign. I don't need to bother you." To which the woman responded by whispering a welcoming invitation to come on in and an apology that she would be off the phone in a few minutes. Isabelle felt she had no choice but to return to the house, since the woman was on the phone using hand gestures and whispers to communicate with Isabelle while not hanging up on the person on the other end of the phone line. Isabelle went inside the porch and sat down to wait. And that was how Isabelle met Sissy.

Chapter 8

Because of their chance encounter one day soon after the Iowa Caucuses were over and Isabelle had more time, Sissy was upstairs in Isabelle's office having coffee. Though they had only met that day she had knocked Sissy's door, there was an unspoken connection and they both knew it. When Sissy had invited Isabelle to come in and sit down on her porch the day they had met Sissy had just unloaded all her frustrations. Pretty soon she and Sissy had found themselves chatting as if they had been old friends and Isabelle invited Sissy to come up to her new office and have coffee and talk politics. *"Could it really be,"* wondered Isabelle, *"that there is another woman in this county, besides Clarys and I, who cares about politics, social justice and women's issues?"* It could be, indeed, she was to learn.

Sissy was an enigma for the area as it turned out. She had only moved to Lakeshore where she found a house she loved (with crumbling front steps) within the last year. It was a charming little arts-and-crafts style house with a front porch that spanned the width of the house and on which Sissy had left boxes and furniture she had yet to unpack or find a spot for. Peering through the large window, Isabelle had seen a fireplace, chintz covered furniture, stacks of books and milk crates full of what looked like old vinyl records.

Isabelle had learned that day that Sissy had formerly lived and worked in New York for a Fortune 500 company and upon receiving her pink slip in the still recovering economy she found herself back in the midwest where she had grown up. She also found herself lonely, culturally and politically starved, only marginally employed, and missing good coffee and her old liberal east coast life. And it was just good coffee, fresh politics, friendship, and a listening ear that Sissy found when she and Isabelle sat down for coffee in Isabelle's new red lounge room she had fashioned from her old studio office. Isabelle learned that the fact that she had come from the area originally was what had enabled Sissy to adjust at all to what had to feel like a social, cultural, and recreational desert after leaving New York City. Sissy found in Isabelle a kindred spirit. Isabelle found Sissy to be refreshing. She was not just refreshing to talk to but she was refreshing to look at.

Sissy looked like she could have played Anne in Anne of Green Gables. She was small in stature and wore her thick strawberry blond hair in a pony tail.

Sissy had freckles. She wasn't covered in freckles; she was blessed with freckles and she wore them shamelessly and in the most naturally beautiful way. Except for a little eye makeup, she wore no makeup. She was quite simply a beautiful woman. And she was as unpretentious a person in how she dressed as Isabelle would ever want to know. When Isabelle met Sissy she was wearing faded jeans and a plaid shirt over-which she wore a wool cardigan. And for the next 3 or 4 times Isabelle saw her, Sissy would either be wearing the same sweater or maybe a different but equally familiar pull-over … and sometimes over the same plaid shirt. If Isabelle hadn't already been impressed, just observing Sissy being her most natural, authentic and beautiful self would have won Isabelle over.

Isabelle and Sissy got acquainted over cups of Americanas while they listened to the north facing window beside them rattle against the angry northwest wind. Isabelle liked Sissy immediately. She loved her genuineness and hearing her story about what had brought her to Lakeshore.

"So tell me about leaving New York and moving to Lakeshore? Isabelle said as they sipped their coffee.

"Well I was from this are. You may not know that but I actually grew up on a farm just south of Lakeview. I had been living in New York for years of course, so I knew, that it would be an adjustment. But my family needed me and I didn't have a job. I owned my own condo and figured I could rent it and for what it cost me to live here I would come out ahead."

"But why Lakeshore?" Isabelle asked. "Why not Lakeview?

"Oh, this house! I love my old craftsmans house. It

has good bones and character and I could pay cash for it. I gave up a lot, yes. But life here can be so peaceful and serene. I love it here. I don't lock my door when I leave. I leave my keys in the car when I park in front of the post office. You know! I would love to find a job, but there don't seem to be any. What about you? What is it like for you to live here? You just moved here with no connections or family ties, right?"

"It's really hard for me at times." Isabelle said. "I have never felt really included and I really long to live in an urban area. And I have wanderlust, I'm afraid.

"So do you travel?"

"I wish! I feel like I was hard wired to travel, Sissy. My wanderlust has to be as frustrating for Henry as his industriousness is to me. He has to deal with my restlessness and my yearning to go somewhere all the time. And I live with his constant need to be productive. Honestly, if the car is leaving the driveway I want to be in it and I don't need to ask where it's going!"

"You must have travelled a lot growing up."

" No not really. But we would go west to the mountains every year and I loved them. I thought someday I would live out there. And now sometimes when we are driving somewhere and the sun is setting I'll tell Henry to just keep driving into that sunset! I'll say to him we could wake up when the sun is coming up in the mountains. And he just laughs." Isabelle lamented.

"My parents moved five times after I left home so I think I come by this honest. Mom once said that dad would have moved more if it hadn't been for needing to support six kids. And all my siblings travel a lot"

"One of my sisters runs marathons around the world. Another one has hunted in Africa two or three times. And my oldest brother lives out of his Casita. He just has a kayak, a guitar, a fiddle and a thirst for experiences and so he takes to the road and just follows it."

"Do you ever get jealous?" Sissy wanted to know.

"All the time. My youngest brother, I used to change his diapers so that tells you how much younger, just sold his house and moved into a condo in St. Louis. He is always instagramming pictures of him and his wife on bike trails, in coffee shops, out walking to happy hour on Friday night. And I'm usually watching The Antique Roadshow when those pop into my phone. Yea, I get jealous."

"But I know what I traded for. I have four daughters. None of my siblings had more than 2 kids. And because of my daughters I have actually been to Italy, Chile, and Spain so I shouldn't complain. I actually think my greater longing is just for urban life. We give up so much to live here, Sissy."

"Wow you have travelled, though! I mean, Spain?!"

"Yes, and that was Henry's idea. I had spent a long boring winter learning Spanish on line and we were approaching our 30th wedding anniversary so Henry said he guessed we better to go to Spain. He really is a bit of a romantic which makes no sense being German."

"Actually last summer we had a great road trip just going to the Black Hills. Henry indulged me went all the way to Rapid City without getting on interstate. It took forever but we had Merle Haggard in the tape deck and the open road and I was loving it!"

Sissy looked out the window and seeing the courthouse and roof tops she exclaimed, "It feels like I'm in a city or something. This is just so cool! I love it up here but I am going to have to go. Thank you so much for this."

As Sissy was leaving, Isabelle suggested that she come back for coffee anytime. "I"ll tell you what," Isabelle said, "If you see my car out front and the beanie baby on the dash is upside down, you'll know I'm not busy and you should come up." Sissy smiled and replied, "Oh, like a speakeasy!" And with that comment, followed by their laughter, Sissy departed. But she left behind the solution for the library table that had been sitting in the entry way at home. Isabelle's longed for coffee shop was going to become a reality and it might just be the

perfect place for activists to meet around a table that

had not yet lost its usefulness after all.

Chapter 9

Isabelle's feelings of desperation from living in Lakeshore for 30 years had resulted in her recognizing and accepting what she could not change and being innovative with what she could change. She had, because of her yearning to travel, become an AIRBNB host for no other reason than to broaden her cultural exposure. "If I can't travel to experience other cultures, I'll bring them to me," Isabelle had said to Henry shortly after she and Henry had returned from Spain where they had stayed in their first AIRBNB. So Isabelle spent some time reading about how to be an AIRBNB host afterwhich she proceeded to set up her own host account with three listings. From their five bedroom house, Isabelle selected three rooms to list. They included Sammy's room, Andy's room and her cabin themed basement room all listed as 1917 arts-and-craft style rooms in the breadbasket of America. She emptied closets and dresser drawers, found an unused blank book to use for a journal, and placed some brochures for nearby tourist destinations. She had a few coffee table books about Iowa that she put on the night stands. Then she bought some white bathrobes, a few decorative pillows, and new sheets and towels.

Once her listings were completed and activated she was sheepishly telling a few locals about her new venture. Of course they thought she was crazy letting perfect strangers spend the night in her house. Often someone would suggest that she should keep a loaded gun ready just in case, a comment she totally expected from people whose fears drove their political positions and love of their 2nd amendment rights. Others couldn't understand why anyone would want to make extra work for themselves with the cleaning, laundry and cooking breakfast. Most of them of course just said "What's an AIRBNB?" Which to Isabelle was enough said. She was starving for stimulation and conversations that went beyond the weather or the local gossip. It was a banner day if she could make a local think she was bat shit crazy.

But her idea turned out to not be crazy. She actually began to receive inquiries and book guests. She had guests from Kansas one of whom was blind but working with her husband's assistance on a book about the role of women during the civil war. They were staying with her because of the nearby library they wanted to visit. She had a couple from New York who were trailering their Harley Davidson to Sturgis and wanted a rural experience with plenty of free parking. "You have no worries there!" Isabelle had told them. She hosted a geotechnical engineer who worked on the San Andreas fault in California but had grown up in Scotland, received his education in Canada and was bringing his daughter to Iowa to enroll her in nursing school. He stayed a week.

One couple she ended up hosting, after first declining them, was a couple from Minnesota. The woman identified herself as a spiritualist which was the deal breaker at first for Isabelle who didn't want anyone trying to wake up ghosts or mess with her head. Then, having scolded and reminded herself that she was doing this for the experiences she would have, Isabelle decided to accept their request and she was not disappointed. They left her with a bread recipe and an invitation to stay with them if Henry and she were ever travelling through their area.

One of her most recent and favorite guests was a woman by the name of Sharon who had brought along her boyfriend. He shared that he had been deployed to Kuwait twice and on the day of their departure they lingered at the breakfast table until 11:00 while he opened up talked about his experiences as a troop on the ground in a hot spot of engagement. Sharon sent Isabelle a message the day after they left telling Isabelle she had not heard him open up about Kuwait to anyone else but her and it had been two years since he had talked about it at all.

Isabelle's guests were always warmly greeted and escorted to their room where fresh baked cookies and bottled water had been placed on their dresser. They would be shown the bathroom smelling of bleach with polished chrome fixtures and spotless mirrors. They would be fed breakfasts cooked by

Henry that might be a frittata, eggs benedict, or sometimes waffles and would often include fresh breads baked by Isabelle to be enjoyed with an Americana or an espressos hand pulled from their espresso machine. With all of their guests Isabelle and Henry would respect their privacy but invite them for wine and conversation after they settled in. And they almost always accepted. And without exception, Isabelle and Henry were entertained. Although their guest reviews made them worthy of super host status they just never could get enough guests in a single AIRBNB review cycle to achieve it. Nevertheless, it was a feather in Isabelle's cap to have the pleasure of her guest's company and an affirmation of her hosting skills reflected in their online reviews or the guest journal they wrote in.

Sometimes after their departure a guest would send her a gift. One sent sheet music having played

Isabelle's baby grand piano. Another sent her a copy of a book she had written. An early guest for whom Isabelle had stretched the rules a bit left her an extra $20 in the journal along with a promise to return someday. Isabelle had with some hesitation let that guest smoke her herbal cigarettes on the deck. *"Wouldn't that be a great headline in the local paper!"* Isabelle thought, thinking (but not knowing), that herbal was probably code for weed. *"Pott's AIRBNB is Busted for Pot*

So having already shown herself to be adept at creating her own happy place in Lakeshore, it really didn't take long for the speak-easy comment from Sissy to morph in Isabelle's mind into a doable idea for a coffee shop. Though the idea of a coffee shop had always intrigued her, Isabelle knew two things; there was no way a small community could support a real coffee shop, and Isabelle didn't want to be stuck working at anything that would cause her to lose the flexibility she enjoyed in her job with the florists. *"But what might work,"* thought Isabelle, *"is a different kind of coffee shop"*. Like AIRBNB had enabled Isabelle to host interesting guests in her home, and like uber had opened opportunities for people to earn extra money in their off time, with simply a smart phone app, using social media there might be a pathway to a speakeasy off-the-radar coffee shop. And, after giving it a measure of thought, Isabelle concluded, *"there most certainly is!"* All she needed was a private Facebook page and members on that page who were on board and wanted good coffee. And with that idea, Isabelle went to a few key people and pitched her idea.

"You see." said Isabelle, "we will keep this private. And we will use my office space. And we will have people we choose join. Everyone will bring their own cup and make their own coffee and we can have discussions about interesting things like politics and religion and women's issues and progress! There will be wifi," said Isabelle, "because I already pay for it anyway. And I'll keep my office but I will separate it from the coffee shop so people don't feel like they're intruding on my personal space. I want people to feel comfortable and feel like they are in a coffee shop. We will all sell club memberships and we will issue punch cards for cups of coffee. That way we won't be selling coffee and violating any health laws! And we'll post on our private page every morning when we open and every afternoon when we close. And if I have to be gone, then, well, we'll be closed! But I'm here almost all the time! And, and, and ..." Isabelle would continue with growing enthusiasm to each of her contacts. She wandered into the boutique to pitch it to her personal shoppers,

Carmen and Mary. And into the newspaper office to

run it by their ad department head, whom Isabelle

knew loved coffee too and was a fair and pragmatic

person whose opinion Isabelle valued. And across

the street to the florist who was a past president of

the local chamber of commerce. And to her lawyer

daughters Andy, May and Sammy who were quick

to say, "Be careful, mom."

"How can this not work?" she asked each of them.

"What is to keep this from working even if we only

have 10 members?" she asked. And no one had an

answer for why it wouldn't work. In fact, no one

really discouraged Isabelle from giving it a try.

Though she saw skepticism in their eyes, their tepid

responses were "Well you can try." and " Why

not?" But there was one person who became

absolutely elated at the idea and that person was

Clarys. And THAT was all Isabelle needed. That, the table from the entryway, a few pieces of equipment, some organization and a little work.

Over the next few weeks, Isabelle and Clarys shifted from political campaigning to playing house and opening a coffee shop. Isabelle set up a Facebook page, invited members, posted a Q & A about how it would work, found a local kid to be the coffee bean roaster, and chatted up random people she planned to invite. Her nights were sleepless. She would wake in the middle of the night feeling like a schoolgirl setting up a lemonade stand or worried about breaking the law with no health safety certificate. But then the sun would rise and the work and the excitement would continue.

She and Clarys scavenged through stored art Clarys wanted to share for the coffee shop walls. They gathered teapots and espresso cups, puzzles and decks of cards, and some twinkle lights for shelving. They had membership cards made, put up a small book exchange shelf, hung a blackboard for posting garden produce sharing items, and labeled and arranged canisters of beans. Isabelle setup the facebook page creating a Q & A to pin to the homepage explaining to group members why they were added to the group.

And then one day in early March, it was time to go real. It was time to start adding people to the facebook page and making coffee, albeit with a limp along cheap grinder, a few pour over funnels, some donated gallons of water and some borrowed tea pots. It was showtime for the Upstairs coffee shop!

At first it was slow. Isabelle noticed that she was the only one adding anyone to the Facebook group. And though she would be despondent over it, she refused to give up. She persevered adding and removing members of the Facebook group as they ignored the idea or showed up with curiosity and their money. And by June the upstairs coffee shop had grown from five members to 25. And with each new member there was another 25 dollars to spend. And eventually they had enough money, to add an *electric* moka pot, a burr coffee grinder, three french presses, a frother, a blender, an assortment of teas, a couple of electric water kettles, and then *another* electric moka pot. But the best part was that they were adding members. Isabelle was beginning to feel optimistic that she was finding her community, something she had never felt she had found in the 30 years she had lived in Lakeshore and in the six years she had worked in Lakeview. Somewhere in those 25 members would be the political activist she was looking for.

Isabelle was feeling so good about things that one night she called her best friend from high school to tell her about it. "Remember the town girls club I started in 2nd grade?" she asked. Her friend reminded her that she had been a country girl and hadn't been invited, making them both laugh. "Well, I know I told you about it! Remember, I made everyone give me a dime and then I bought the teacher a petunia? And I got to be the president and the treasurer and everyone had to do what I said? And it was only for the town girls because the country girls had their own club ... don't you remember?" Isabelle reminded her friend of the story and then said, "Well, I'm doing it again. I'm opening a coffee shop and I get to decide who joins, how much the membership is and everything else. And here's the funny part," she said, "If they complain, I can just punch them out!" Of course

Isabelle meant that she could buy out their card but she loved saying she could punch them out.

And so the coffee shop was born. Isabelle was using coffee and a table to bring people together who would come to color the upstairs. She never had to punch anyone out. She had created the intimate spaces for conversations and reading and working that Lakeview lacked and she had thirsted for. She hadn't done it to be bossy. She had done it because she needed it and thought others did too and she had figured out a way to make it happen. And little by little she was seeing people's lives change. As they joined and Isabelle shared her story of loneliness that had led her to the idea of opening the coffee shop, they were sharing their own stories. It was amazing to Isabelle how many people in this tight little community were feeling isolated and lonely. She was amazed out how many of them who had lived in the community for decades echoed Isabelle's experience of never having been embraced by the community or felt welcome by the residents whose families had been farming and living in Lakview for generations and had no idea they were behaving exclusively. She was seeing joy in people she had barely known before. They were thanking her and expressing disbelief at how they felt upstairs. Some of them were finding refuge. Some were finding camaraderie. Some were escaping reality or just re-charging their batteries in a hidden secret place where no one was likely to even know where they were. But all of them were connecting. They were all feeling a sense of belonging and Isabelle was forming a community. And it was feeling good.

Chapter 10

The upstairs members who joined seeking camaraderie was a woman by the name of Harmony. Harmony was a Lutheran pastor who made a joyful noise as she would whistle and sing her way down the hallway. Isabelle was working in her office one day when she heard the heavy front door bang shut followed by the sound of someone's footsteps coming down the hall. She had only just added Harmony to the Facebook group the night before after a request from her. Then that morning with her "OPEN" post Harmony had responded that she would be coming but it wouldn't be until after Wait Wait Don't Tell Me was over. "W*ell score one for her,*" thought Isabelle. "*You can't be all bad if you listen to public radio*". As the sound of footsteps drew closer Isabelle walked out to see who it was, only to run face to face into Harmony the pastor.

Harmony was wearing loose jeans and floral crocks and she was carrying her knitting, an I-pad and a book. Strapped across her torso was a fringed leather shoulder bag with a peace sign on it. It had well deserved patina from all appearances. "S*he's was a little 'out there,*" thought Isabelle, in spite of the starched white collar under her starched black shirt that was circled by a drapey silk scarf that Isabelle had to wonder about. "*A few tugs on the ends of that scarf,*" thought Isabelle, "*and the white collar could just disappear underneath it and no one would ever know. I wonder ....*" Harmony's face was young and her skin was smooth and beautiful. She had delicate features and a lovely smile that she shared generously and despite herself,

Isabelle suspected she might be able to over-look the collar in this woman of the cloth.

Isabelle recalled having heard about Harmony a few years ago from Henry when Harmony had first moved to Lakeview and Henry had treated one of her animals. Harmony had mentioned to Henry that she was a knitter and a weaver. At that time, Isabelle was meeting weekly with a few friends and knitting. They would do a fair amount of gossiping, venting and quite a bit of swearing . When Henry came home and told Isabelle that she might want to reach out to this new person Isabelle just about freaked out. Assuring her that he hadn't shared anything about the knitting club, Isabelle was relieved. The one thing she and her friends did not need was suppression of their weekly venting sessions because a pastor was present!

But a coffee shop is not a bitch club and Isabelle

was eager to grow memberships and find her community of activists so when Harmony and she met upstairs Isabelle was her most cordial self.

" Hi, I'm Isabelle," Isabelle said in greeting. "You must be Harmony. I've heard about you. Welcome to the upstairs coffee shop. So you are interested in maybe joining our coffee co-op?"

"I brought my money", Harmony responded.

A bit taken aback at the abrupt disclosure of Harmony's apparent decision to join already, Isabelle nonetheless left that comment just dangling and proceeded to explain how the coffee shop was uniquely modeled with members making their own artisan coffee, doing their own cash only business, bringing and washing their own cup, and then ended with "So it may not be your thing." Upon which Harmony reached into her fringed bag and pulled out 25 dollars.

"My son is so excited for me," she said. "I only have one question. Do I get to be a democrat up here?" Which of course she did.

"Bingo!" thought Isabelle. And so Harmony became a member of the co-op. She would often visit with her knitting or her i-pad to work on a sermon. And she almost always brought a book but she was just as willing to converse with whoever else was upstairs and gaze out the window which once elicited the comment, "I just don't feel like I'm in Lakeview when I'm up here."

In time Harmony would prove to be a frequent visitor upstairs. Though she would invoke God in conversation she was just as likely to refer to the evangelical Christian Zionists as crazies. She would educate the members who were interested about the history of Palestine and the Palestinian people. As a pastor her political and social justice interests put her at risk of being ostracized by the community which was why she grew very protective of the upstairs coffee shop. Often she would caution Isabelle about letting too many people know about the upstairs. Isabelle was fully aware that Harmony loved its privacy, obscurity and liberal vibe, causing her to constantly assure Harmony that she was quite capable of managing the upstairs membership. Isabelle would say, "After All, Harmony. I have been known to keep a pastor out of a knitting club, you know!"

Harmony would become a very important member of the upstairs. And months later Harmony would prove how important upstairs had been to her. She came for escape and solace. She came to be in a place where she could speak to her liberal views and to discuss issues about which she was passionate. She brought members insight and knowledge that she shared about the Palestinian oppression by the Israelis. But sadly, when in the coming months the community discovered her liberal leanings and no longer wanted her, Harmony looked to the friendships she had formed through her upstairs membership to help her depart Lakeview. But that would wait. For now, Harmony had a community and a place. She had found camaraderie and made new friends, not the least of which was her new friend Connie.

Chapter 11

Connie had been invited to the coffee shop because knowing that she was a freelance journalist who traveled and worked from home, Isabelle figured she would love having a place where she could go work with wifi access and good coffee and she had figured right. Connie joined upstairs and would often show up with her laptop to spend 3 or 4 hours quietly writing at the little bistro table.

Connie and Harmony both fit much better into the community of Lakeview that Isabelle found so oppressive because of its Christian extremism. Isabelle had been raised in a much more moderate protestant community thus experiencing culture shock at the frequent witnessing to each other among the members of the communities, something

Connie was used to as a native of Stone County, the constant references to God in the most casual conversations, such as "It was God's plan" or "I'll pray for you." Isabelle would cringe inside when she heard those comments but Connie seemed oblivious.

Religion defined Connie and Harmony. Connie was a faithful servant to her church in a nearby town so small there was not even a post office. And in her church they allowed Connie to run the show, at least with the Christian Education program. That suited her just fine. Connie preferred to be in charge and she would be the first to admit she preferred to run things without the distraction of helpers who would only make her inefficient and waste her time proving to them her way was the best way.

Connie was a confident woman. She had the kind of confidence that might come off to others as narcissistic at first. But given time, Isabelle would learn that it was only an impression and not really an accurate one at all. It was just such a first impression that had caused Isabelle to keep Connie a bit at arm's length, that is until she opened her coffee shop. Thanks to upstairs, Isabelle would learn more about Connie and get to know her better and she would discover that Connie's apparent narcissism was not that at all. It was really just a survival tool developed by Connie as an outcome of having worked in a good old boys club for so many years.

She worked for an agricultural company ghost writing articles for lesser educated men with titles who didn't mind putting their name on her work. Or if they actually wrote something, Connie would come along behind them and clean up their articles before they went to print. Years of being a victim of manterrupting and mansplanations had made Connie a feminist. After getting to know her better, it became clear to Isabelle that Connie had had to develop some survival behaviors and arm herself with confidence and assertiveness so that when she was the smartest person in a room full of over confident men with titles, she could utilize that confidence to intimidate them. The problem was that she was so good at it, she often put off or intimidated women too, which is why Isabelle suspected after her disclosure of feeling isolated too, that Connie was lonely. So Isabelle and Clarys became Connie's new friends and when the opportunity came to introduce her to Harmony, knowing they were both strong women who shared deep faith, Isabelle connected them.

Though she was in her mid 60's, Connie was as blond as a native Scandinavian. She stood all of 5 feet 4 inches tall and often wore red polka dot high top shoes with wild leggings and long tops. Every Thursday afternoon Connie would run a little faith based Sesame Street at her church. She would get to teach morals, color pictures, give kids snacks and for 2 hours a week run the world, where running the world really mattered. Isabelle suspected that when they needed her, she helped in the church kitchen too, but there were plenty of women to run the church kitchen. You didn't have to know her well or very long to correctly conclude that Connie was much better utilized by her church in teaching and molding young minds, than in arguing with the church circle ladies about how to organize the church kitchen and whether to store the hundreds of saved cool whip containers in the big deep drawer under the table cloths or in the cabinet above the coffee cups. Connie had been teaching church school for 40 years no doubt taking full advantage of her position to teach a little tolerance and acceptance to young formative minds. Isabelle had no idea if she was appreciated, but from her perspective the church was lucky to have Connie. And so was Isabelle and the upstairs. *"Score five?"* thought Isabelle when Connie joined upstairs. Members like Connie gave upstairs depth and complexity. Thankfully there were other members who brought sunshine. And that would include Ki.

Chapter 12

Ki was a petite Asian woman who not only contributed to the diversity of the upstairs but also just spread joy wherever she went. Isabelle would often wish Ki would sit down to drink her coffee, but Ki was always in a hurry. She would run up the stairs every morning about the same time to make her take-away cold press. Isabelle would hear her quick, heavy footsteps as she hurried down the hall knowing without even having to look that it was Ki. Looking out her office door Isabelle would see her head bop up as she neared the top of the steps and immediately be brightened by her cheery smile and her brightly colored signature headband. Ki always held her black hair back with wide floral headbands and she must have owned a hundred of them.

"Ki! You can't weigh more than 100 pounds! But you walk like a full back!" Isabelle said one day when she stepped out of her office nearly colliding with Ki.

"That's what everyone tells me." Ki replied. "My husband says I'm the densest person he knows, though."

Ki was definitely an athletic type. To use the saying of Isabelle's father that she was built like a brick shit-house would have been a bit of a stretch, but she was as solid a woman as Isabelle had ever known. Besides running everywhere she went, she had been doing yoga for years. Ki did yoga before most northern Iowans had figured out it wasn't a religion that needed to be banned like the Harry Potter books. In the summer she would do a lot of paddle boarding, kayaking, bicycling, and motorcycle riding with her husband with whom she would head west to hike and drink beer every summer. No one loved beer as much as Ki and she knew beer like Isabelle knew coffee. Isabelle loved hearing her stories about hiking all day with her husband before finding themselves a good cozy bar at the end of the day where they would park themselves to drink good beer and watch her beloved Yankees.

One day Ki came in and Isabelle was wandering aimlessly around trying to find her reading glasses.

"They're on your head," said Ki looking up from measuring out her cream for her sweet cream cold press.

"Geesh!" Isabelle said. "This morning I couldn't find my favorite lipstick and Henry found it in the refrigerator. And it's my favorite color that Kohl's quit carrying. So I can't afford to misplace it."

"You should buy my lipstick. I can mix you any color you want," said Ki.

So a few weeks later Ki came upstairs with her samples and an hour later left with $57 of Isabelle's money. Isabelle was happy and Ki was happy. Isabelle never could get a read on Ki's politics. She held her views closer than anyone Isabelle had ever known.

Chapter 13

Many followers of the upstairs Facebook group never were able to join the co-op. They included some of the member's children or Isabelle's friends who were so enamored by the whole concept that every so often Isabelle would pick up her mail and find a package from one of them. There was the time she got handcrafted tea made in Kansas from an admirer in Wichita of the coffee cooperative idea. Then there was the florist friend who sent chicory coffee from New Orleans. And there was the pilot friend who having made a quick flight to Costa Rica picked up some beans and shipped them to Isabelle. Isabelle was always so touched by such random acts of generosity.

One non member in particular had the unique role

of roasting most of the beans for upstairs. Rocky was just a young kid of 25 who had dreams including to someday have his own coffee shop. Upstairs was the beneficiary of his passion for coffee. He had acquired a coffee roaster so he could roast his own beans. When Isabella heard about it she asked him to roast for her. Rocky would roast a batch of beans and deliver them whenever Isabelle messaged him that beans were getting low. He usually made time to chat with Isabelle about his life ... balancing work life and lifestyle choices, politics, travel and relationships, and almost anything else he would want her opinion on. Rocky never had to pay for a membership or punch a card upstairs. Isabelle granted him privileged status just for contributing the unique component to a Lakeview coffee house of offering locally roasted beans. Isabelle knew that Rocky would move on someday and the local roast boast would leave with him but she hoped it would be a very long time before that happened. Rocky was a free spirit who brought charm to the upstairs. Rocky had a girl and a dog and he was clearly deeply and passionately in love with and devoted to them both. Isabelle had seen pictures of his girlfriend and she was drop dead gorgeous, which made her a good match for Rocky who was pretty gorgeous himself. Isabelle hoped that if they ended up together she would still know them when they made what promised to be gorgeous babies. In the meantime she enjoyed Rocky's beans and his company, and knew he would never be part of her activist group even though he would have been a great addition.

One of the members upstairs was the toymaker, Lars a Libertarian Ex Hippie and heart attack survivor, who would often drag up someone from his shop to introduce them to Isabelle. The day he brought Jay was a red letter day. Jay brought not just gender balance but he brought outside cultural experiences to share with upstairs. Jay was a nice looking intelligent man who had spent most of his adult life in China where he worked for a New York real estate company. Jay's job was to network and shake out money from wealthy Chinese investors. He had some shared history with Clarys and they would enjoy talking about the unrest of the 70's when Clarys was in California and Jay was at the University of Iowa. They were both part of the civilian resistance of the decade. One day Jay brought in some yellowed 1970 and 1971 newspapers called "The Militant". Isabelle enjoyed them many quiet afternoons on cold winter days when it seemed no one was drinking coffee anymore. Jay was the mystery member. Or at least to some of the women members he was suspect. It was amusing to Isabelle to listen to them discuss their theories on what such a good looking guy was *really* doing in China! they would speculate about whether he was truly an international business man, or a womanizer, or drug dealer. It was suggested that he must be a recovering alcoholic. It really didn't matter to Isabelle. He was a coffee shop member of the male gender with an interest in politics, an interesting background and a stimulating conversationalist. Whatever else he was, was just frosting on the cake in her view.

And so the coffee shop was peopled. What had started as a blank slate, like the blackboard on its wall, came to be colored by the members that graced it with their presence. And it became Isabelle's happy place where she would go every day to work and find friendship and diversion from the reality she found herself in in Lakeview. With the caucuses being over in Iowa the long wait had begun for the party conventions and the decision about who the candidate would be. For the first time in a long time, Isabelle was feeling more happy and fulfilled than she had for a very long time. She felt like she was finding her community and building a network of liberal advocates who were empowering each other. She felt purposeful again. That was a good thing for her and Henry and Story County.

Chapter 14

It was going to be a warm June day. With temperatures forecasted to be in the 90's and storms predicted to be moving in by late afternoon, Isabelle had come to work in one of her favorite sun dresses. This morning she had not changed clothes three times as usual. She had in fact gone to bed with her orange sundress already laid out. She had selected her wildest purple floral head band and paired it with some large Spanish style earrings reminiscent of an Aztec sun. To finish her ensemble she put on her Birkenstock sandals, mostly because anyone else would have matched the outfit with something strappy and elevated like espadrilles which she didn't have.

Isabelle checked the temperature about nine o'clock after she had arrived at the coffee shop and it was already 80 degrees. Though she was tempted to open the window for some fresh air she knew no one else would appreciate it. She told Henry she waited all winter for the kind of warm humid air that wraps itself around you in the summer and warms your bones, so at home she kept windows open. At the coffee shop, not so much.

Isabelle was sitting at her desk when she heard the front door close and then foot steps approaching her office door. She looked up as Lars passed by.

"What's up?" Isabelle asked him.

"Not much." Lars said. "I came to pick your brain."

Lars seemed to like Isabelle's take on most subjects because she was usually non-conforming and her responses amused him. Lars was one of those guys that you could tell by looking at him he was a pot stirrer, and maybe smoker! Isabelle didn't see herself as a rebel; maybe she was a non-conformist but she certainly didn't see herself in the same league as Lars. She did admire dissidents though, and suspecting that Lars had done his share of dissenting, Isabelle was equally interested in what Lars had to say. She followed him into the coffee shop.

"Where are all the people? Lars asked as he made his hot tea.

"Good question! I don't know, Lars. Some days I think I'm the only one in this town that wants a coffee shop. I know it's hot out and I've been gone but Henry unlocked this door every day and as far as I have been able to tell no one has been here. All week."

"People go to the bar to talk to the bartender. If you're not here they probably haven't been."

"That may be but I'm worried we have pissed some of the members off. I think they might be picking up a liberal vibe when they're up here that they don't like and don't want to be a part of.

"Ya, think?" Lars replied. "Isn't that what this is all about?"

"Yes, but I want this to be our Algonquin. I want discourse and idea exchanges. I don't want this coffee shop to be just an echo chamber. But name me one person in this whole town, just one, that voted for Trump or King that would be willing to talk to us and explain why. Just one!" Isabelle slumped in her chair and sighed.

"Can't think of anyone," Lars said. "I think we might be the two smartest people in this town. Have you got time for me to pick your brain?"

"Ha! Go for it Lars. See where it gets ya! What's up?"

"I'm looking for $300,000. Any idea who has that much money?"

"Well lots of people but why would they give it to you?

"Because this town needs an injection of energy and no one is doing anything about it and I have an idea. We need to buy that old theatre across the street and fix it up. We could have an artists community in this town if we just got our rears in gear! We need maker space and an entrepreneurial lab for our young people. We should be having musical events by local talented musicians. I'm looking for a grant."

" Don't you go bringing any government entitlement money into our town, Lars. You know we hate entitlement programs around here! Uh … where do we start? I'm in."

"I'll get back to you," Lars said. I just wanted to know if you were on board.

"I would be happy to help. And I would suggest you play the poverty/suicide/chemical dependency card when you apply. Put some data to it. It's out there and we can lay claim to plenty of bad statistics that should make us perfect recipients for some grant money that would address those issues. I'll help write it if you want." Isabelle said.

A few days later Isabelle stopped in to see Lars in his shop. She was baking a coffee cake upstairs and she needed some cooking spray. Lars actually lived in the basement below his toy shop so when you went in you might have to yell for him if you didn't see him. Isabelle opened the door.

Immediately the smell of wood shavings wafted up from the floor confirming she was in a woodworkers shop. The shelves along the walls displayed trains, puzzles, baby rattles, and little cars and trucks all made out of wood. Light streaming in the window captured billions of tiny dust particles that seemed to stay magically suspended as they danced in the air. Imagining she was at the North Pole was easy.

The floor was slippery covered in sawdust making it easy to also imagine someone falling down or a fire. More than once Isabelle had used her foot to stamp out a fire on the floor. The saws on full display would get heated up when Lars was working. And he worked where his customers, and their children stood right beside them as he turned out a wand or a wheel.. Being right in the middle of the workshop was part of the charm but Isabelle had to wonder about Lars' liability insurance and if his agent had ever visited his shop.

"Lars, you here?" Isabelle shouted.

"I'm in here?" Lars yelled back.

"It's Isabelle. Are you behind the red curtain?"

"Yeah, come on back!"

With some trepidation, Isabelle pulled back the curtain. Standing at what might have been a mid-century gas stove was Lars, frying slabs of cottage bacon for his breakfast. Surrounding him were pans, dishes, food products, utensils, and all sorts of things cluttering every surface in what best could be described as a hoarder's galley kitchen. Two very large and very full plastic garbage cans sat against a wall to Lars' back when he stood at his stove. Between him and the cans was a narrow path to an escape out the back. There was no table or chairs that Isabelle could remember after she left but there had been so much to take in she wasn't really sure. Isabelle asked if she could have some cooking spray, quickly sprayed her pan, and then made a hasty exit.

"Come up for some coffee cake this afternoon if you're interested," she said as she left out the front door.

Isabelle went back to her own kitchen to finish her coffee cake thinking about what she had just seen. It made her kind of sad.

Lars was about 60 years old and he stood all of five feet four inches tall. He was all alone having never been married and when Isabelle once asked him why he said he guessed he had just been lucky. He seemed happy, even claimed to be the happiest person he knew, but Isabelle did wonder. Lars had survived a heart attack over a decade ago and told her once that he was bi-polar. Soon after he recovered from this heart attack he intentionally reinvented himself. He walked away from a pressure cooker software engineering job in another state, put on a pair of jeans, a plaid flannel shirt, wide red suspenders and moved home. He stopped drinking, stopped cutting his hair and started making toys. He opened his little shop with a child size gnome on the awning to trademark himself and proceeded to get himself into the world wide web. He knew how to do that. His guest book included people from all over the world and he brought many of them upstairs for a complimentary cup of coffee. Isabelle loved it. Because of him she and anyone else upstairs met traveling musicians, film makers, writers, their mystery international businessman and random average travelers from random average places looking for not so average experiences.

 Lars would not become part of her political activist group but he would bring great conversation and perspective to the table and he inspired and entertained the members. And he was the champion community activist who made a difference every day to someone he met. *"And if he could reinvent Lakeview, more power to him,"* Isabelle thought.

Chapter 15

One humid night in late June Isabelle was sitting out on hers and Henry's shaded deck having a glass of wine alone. Isabelle often had her happy hour alone. Henry would get home from work about five but he would always go right to his garden and work another hour or so. It was his golf. It was his bar time, he would say.

Coming up the drive with a five gallon bucket of Romas, Henry spotted Isabelle on the deck.

"Did you pour me a glass?" Henry asked.

"No, but if you're not just passing through, I will," Isabelle wished Henry would just come home from work and be done for the day but she was glad he didn't golf or go to the bar and watch Jeopardy with the guys so she didn't complain. Much.

"I could stand to sit down for a bit. It took me an hour to pick these. I can't imagine those immigrant workers that do this all day."

Isabelle poured Henry his wine and looked skeptically at the bucket of tomatoes.

"Do you think any of your coffee shop members would want a few of these?" Henry asked. He knew that Isabelle was done freezing, roasting, and canning tomatoes for them.

"I can take a box full." Isabelle said. "I can see some of them wanting a few. What's going to happen with your garden when we go on vacation?"

Henry and Isabelle were planning a week away to do some driving and hiking in the canyons of southern Utah in a week. It was the second year in a row they had taken a vacation. Isabelle recalled their discussion in the car recently when she had commented about missing annual vacations since Ivy had left home.

"Are you forgetting our trips to Chicago and our trip to Spain?" Henry had asked incredulously. "Are you forgetting our AMTRAK vacation to Glacier National Park?"

"I'm talking *vacation*. Not trips. A vacation is something you do in the car and requires *Coleman* things," she had said. "Like our *Coleman* lantern, our *Coleman* sleeping bags, our *Coleman* camp stove. A trip is extra. A vacation is *annual*. I'm beginning to see what the problem is!"

"I think maybe I am too!" Henry said as he smiled across the seat at her.

Isabelle knew that the amount of travel they could enjoy wasn't going to change in the near future. Henry was not going to be taking more time off for a long time. So ultimately Isabelle would sigh a long internal sigh and resign herself to making life the best it could be in the place that she was.

The next morning Isabelle hauled the box of tomatoes to the coffee shop and lugged them up the steps hoping she wouldn't be carrying them back down that night. She posted her location to upstairs facebook page and then filled an empty wine bottle with water for her geranium in the hallway window..

Isabelle took a minute to gaze out the window across the top of the roof of the Farm Bureau at the co-op elevators. The sky was a beautiful blue and there wasn't a cloud in it. The sun was already high but still front-lighting the white elevators against a deep blue sky creating a signature Iowa landscape that caught Isabelle's photographic eye. She decided to try to capture an image of it for the upstairs Facebook page. She picked up her smart phone and positioned it at an angle liking the architecture of the building in the foreground and the way it pulled the viewer into the picture. It was beautiful in a rural skyscraper kind of way so she decided to post it captioned "a rooftop view from the speak easy sidewalk," and also remembered to post that there were free roma tomatoes upstairs.

The upstairs didn't really have a sidewalk of course. A sidewalk would have been her preference for the coffee shop but a private-speakeasy-cooperative-coffee-club couldn't have a table on the main street sidewalk in such a small town. For one thing it would mean the speakeasy was no longer a speakeasy and for another thing, most people would just be annoyed and think someone was being a bit

hoity toity to sit outside to drink a cup of coffee as

if there wasn't work to do like there was for

everyone else. *"As if I care"*, thought Isabelle. The

bigger reason there could be no sidewalk bistro

table was the god awful wind that swept across

northwest Iowa. Wind gusts could often be so

strong that they might blow an umbrella right out of

its stand or blow chairs down main street. So

instead, Isabelle had put two stools and a small table

by a south facing window in the long hall that led to

the coffee shop when one reached the top of the

stairs. She had found a vintage cloth to drape over

the table and with a red geranium in a cobalt blue

ceramic pot set in the deep window sill, something

about it seemed very European making Isabelle

happy. Never mind no one ever sat there. And never

mind her arrogant brother who saw the image of

her speakeasy sidewalk table had asked if she was living in an Amish prison camp. It made Isabelle happy and that was enough.

Isabelle's phone chimed a notification as she was sitting down at her desk.

"You there?" the message said.

"Yep. All day." Isabelle texted back.

It was Tuesday morning after the long July fourth weekend and Isabelle hadn't seen Clarys in almost a week. Typically when they were both home, they would see each other daily at the coffee shop. Isabelle loved that but she always felt bad thinking that Clarys might enjoy coming to the upstairs with just a book or her laptop for a change and she would suggest that Clarys should do that and feel like she could use the coffee shop like she would any other coffee shop where she might go to just lose herself in a book and not feel obligated to visit with anyone. But Clarys would always respond, "Oh no! I came to visit with you!" So Isabelle and she would sit and talk for a few hours sometime doing so as often as a couple of times a week.

But on this post holiday morning when Clarys texted and said she was coming to the coffee shop Isabelle intentionally left to go to the post office anyway . In spite of what Clarys had said about coming to visit with her, she wanted to give Clarys the coffee shop for a while by herself even if for only the few minutes it took her to walk to the post office and back. Which is what she intended to do. But as was common, Isabelle stuck her head in the door of the boutique as she walked passed it to say good morning to her friends Carmen.

Isabelle had first met Carmen and Mary when she had opened her studio. Carmen had booked a sitting for her five grandchildren, all under five years of age. Isabelle remembered it as the job from hell. It had been clear from the start that lining up five kids under six with crossed ankles and cherubic smiles was not in the realm of reality. But after some 150 random shots of attempting to arrange them in a semblance of order, she had finally thrown out a bunch of plastic Easter eggs hoping it would keep them in one place long enough to get some decent shots. It had worked. She had managed to grab some shots of them playing with the eggs and for the most part they were all at least facing the camera. It was the best she could do considering the illegality of sedating them, and she was ultimately pleased. She had even been able to crop out some individual shots from the group shot since none of the kids were touching each other. So when all was said and done, she had a set of proofs to present to

Carmen with no shame or apology, other than that she was sorry she hadn't provided wine for the adults in the room. The shoot would turn out to be a bonding experience between the three women; one they would remember over the years with laughter.

At about that same time as their meeting for shooting the grandkids, Carmen and Mary opened their clothing boutique. When the boutique opened just a few stores down the street from her then studio Isabelle's shopping habits changed pretty dramatically. Suddenly she had convenience, affordability, and manageable inventory converging in one place less than 100 steps from her studio. Along with getting Carmen and Mary as her personal shoppers, Isabelle was suddenly in retail heaven and no longer overwhelmed by too many choices.

For Isabelle, it didn't matter whether it was a

supermarket or a department store. She always appreciated being able to spend 15 minutes buying a week's worth of groceries for a family of six in Lakeshore's pretty good grocery where you had only two choices of brands and four aisles of groceries. Nevermind you couldn't buy avocados, green onions, or blueberries just any day you wanted to. And never mind she lived in a town where you couldn't buy a pair of nylons on Sunday. Isabelle really did appreciate buying her essential groceries locally where they didn't keep the place so cold that you had to wear a snowmobile suit in July to puruse the limited produce.

Groceries aside, clothing shopping was even more dreaded by Isabelle. Isabelle had purchased her first suit for her job with the florists under force by Henry and her daughters who took her to the store and made her try on clothes. Most of her shopping was mail order because it was so much easier so when Isabelle learned that she had been described by someone as wearing skirts and sweaters and jeans just think L.L.Bean sells she wasn't surprised. Indeed Isabelle could find many L.L. Bean labels in her sweater drawer. She loved sweaters and she loved cold weather which was another trait that made her an enigma in Lakeview where you are supposed to complain about the weather. She told her family to bury her in a wool sweater when she died, even if it was July. That was before she decided to be cremated, of course.

Isabelle recognized the importance of reciprocity in business transactions so not infrequently Isabelle would visit the boutique to browse and buy and then she would end up staying and visiting, sometimes for a half hour, before she felt guilty enough for keeping them from their work that she would make an excuse to keep moving on.. Often she would walk by on her way to the post office or the pretty good thrift store and she would open the door to just say good morning and ask if there was anything new, which is what she had done this morning.

And as usual they chatted far longer than Isabelle had expected. But that was okay, thought Isabelle. It just gave Clarys more time in the coffee shop to be alone. Carmen and Isabelle shared their holiday stories and then Carmen asked if Isabelle had seen Clarys. "She's coming to the coffee shop this morning," Isabelle said, "why?"

"Oh, I'm just worried about her." said Carmen. "I saw one of her friends up at the lakes this weekend and she said that she thought she was depressed and she's worried about her".

Isabelle said that she felt like Clarys was doing fine

and that in fact a number of random people had told her how Clarys had changed since the coffee shop opened, in a good and happy way. Looking at her watch, Isabelle said, "I've gotta get going! Stop up later if you have time." Isabelle left for the post office thinking and wondering what might be up with Clarys.

It had been a rough 48 hours for America. There had been two tragic shootings of purportedly innocent black men profiled and killed by law enforcement which was followed by the shooting of 11 law enforcement officers by a sniper at a peaceful protest in Dallas leaving six of them dead. The stress factor of the entire country was elevated and Facebook posts were all over the map with some supporting men in blue and others proclaiming black lives matter. Everyone was talking about it and it was just the sort of topic that commonly took place upstairs. Upstairs, sometimes saw a spike in coffee drinking on days like this.

As she had gotten to know her better over the months, what Isabelle had learned about Clarys was that she carried the weight of the world around with her all time. She cared genuinely and passionately for those who lived in the margins of society. Clarys had been a social worker before her retirement. And thus she had witnessed some sad and ugly stuff. It didn't help that personally life had been hard for Clarys too. She had lost her mother in her 20's, would go on to marry the wrong man, would raise two daughters in a home under a cloud of alcoholism and spend the rest of her life trying to forgive herself for everything she saw wrong in her life and second guessing herself on every decision she had ever made.

So on the morning after the shootings, Isabelle

knew the weight of the world would be bearing down on Clarys. And if the friend at the lake picking up on her depression even before the shootings was accurate, it was definitely going to be coffee time, thought Isabelle as she headed back upstairs from her errand.

"Hi!" Isabelle said in her cheeriest voice when she saw Clarys sitting at the table. "Sorry, I went to the post office and then stopped in and got delayed talking to Carmen. I was hoping you might enjoy having the shop to yourself a bit!". Isabelle used a fake cheery voice when she thought someone needed it even though no one believed it to be her. Why she continued to do it she had no idea. *She* didn't even like the sound of it. She was much more comfortable with just flippantly but caringly saying "Chin up, buttercup!"

"Oh, no! I came to talk to you", Clarys said. Of

course, Isabelle already knew that but she hadn't yet figured out her therapy approach so she needed to buy some time.

Isabelle went to the kitchen thinking about how best to be the friend Clarys needed today. She could see that Clarys was not put together this morning. Usually she had her makeup on or at least a little lipstick. This morning she didn't even look like she had combed her hair.

Isabelle made herself an iced coffee carefully measuring out five ounces of cold press and three ounces of filtered water. Then she added several ice cubes to a frosted fruit jar and stirred in a little simple syrup. She stalled a little longer putting all her ingredients away and sorting her thoughts before going back out and sitting down to ask Clarys how her weekend had been thinking that would be a way to get Clarys started talking. It was

clear that today the coffee shop conversation was
not going to be about politics.

 Isabelle knew Clarys had been with her sister but
she didn't really know much about Clarys' sister.
She knew about several of Clary's toxic friendships
that could send her into a downward spiral but as far
as Isabelle knew she had not spent the weekend
with any of them. Her strategy was to get Clarys to
talk. About anything at all. And then … wing it.

Isabelle was to learn that Clarys had spent hours on
the phone the previous night with a friend about
whom even Clarys herself acknowledged, was not
good for her. And to make it worse this day was the
birthday of the most toxic of her friends. *"Hmmm"*
thought Isabelle, *"already depressed according to a*
friend, violence on the streets of America, long
night on the phone with a depressed friend, birthday
of a friend that won't speak to her … this is not

looking good. What can I say that will help?"

Though she tried to say all the right things to make

her feel better, it didn't take long before Clarys

basically said she wasn't okay.

"What do you mean, you're not okay?"

"I hate myself and I hate my life. I hate living here.

If it wasn't for you and this coffee shp I would

move."

"How long have you felt this way?"

"I've felt like this for a long time. I've always hated

myself. I can't actually remember when I was

okay".

"Oh, I hate to hear that" Isabelle said feeling so

inadequate. "Find something in yourself to love,

Clarys! You have to do that for yourself. And find

something good in your life. You were the one who

wrote on the upstairs black board 'bloom where you are planted' so take your own advice. I don't think either one of us like it here, Clarys, but this is where we have been planted so this is what we deal with."

Isabelle knew how hard it had been for her to come to terms with Lakeview. It wasn't as if she was always counseling Clarys. Clarys had been there for her many times when she had commiserated over feeling stuck in Lakeview and listing all the things in her life she felt she had no control of including the ticking clock towards old age and not seeing that she would escape Lakeview with her life. It's what drove her to frustration with Henry and made her generally restless. She had made some real strides though in changing her attitude. And that was in part due to Clarys listening and offering comments that Isabelle needed to hear. Even though offering unsolicited advice is never a good idea,

Isabelle decided to take a chance and offer some anyway.

She told Clarys her own story about how she had been able raise herself out of the depths by using her own mother like a mirror whose reflection made Isabelle say to herself she had to get a grip. She told Clarys that the coffee shop chalkboard post of blooming where you are planted was a message she needed to hear and that she thought Clarys had known that when she had decorated the blackboard. And yet, even as she related her own story, Isabelle knew that this wasn't about her and that what Clarys was dealing with was definitely much more real and much deeper than just frustration about living in Lakeview. In fact what concerned Isabelle more than anything was that maybe Isabelle herself was the worst possible person to try to make Clarys feel better. From Clary's perspective, and indeed from those of many in Lakeview, Isabelle had the perfectly charmed life. *"Who wants to hang out with someone who has never met with diversity, poverty, illness, catastrophe, dysfunction or poverty?"* When she thought of that, Isabelle always liked to think they should have met her mother. *"That might give me some credibility in the dysfunction department!"*

"You know, Clarys, it's all going to be okay and tomorrow is another day. Right?" said Isabelle.

"I know. Thanks for listening, friend." Clarys gave Isabelle a hug and headed down the speak easy sidewalk.

"Chin up, buttercup!" Isabelle shouted as she watched Clarys walk away.

A while later after Clarys left, Isabelle couldn't stop thinking about their conversation. Isabelle was frustrated trying to figure out how to help Clarys and what prompted Clarys to be so low. Clarys always seemed to share her personal regrets and stories only to the very edge of the real crux which she carefully protected, leaving Isabelle with big gaps about her past and her demons. So later that week when Carmen sent a text asking if Isabelle had time for coffee, Isabelle said "Yes!" and then grabbed her phone to send a text to Clarys to come for coffee too. She was very relieved to receive a response from Clarys "on my way". *"This is good"*, thought Isabelle. *"I have a back up here and since Clary's is free to join us, between Carmen and me we can make her feel better! We will three all be here now. Everything will work out. It always does with enough coffee and a good cry."*

The three of them, Carmen, Clarys and Isabelle, didn't really get to have coffee together often enough. Between someone being gone or Carmen and Isabelle needing to get work done, or one of them helping a daughter with the grandkids, they had to sneak in random chances to meet upstairs. Luckily, and unluckily more often than not, at least one of them was traveling for fun. They all three loved to travel and would lament how much fun it would be to take a trip together. Carmen was about to spend three weeks in Spain visiting her distant cousins. Clarys was going on a cruise of the Mediterranean in August with her sister-in-law. Isabelle and Henry had gone to Spain for their anniversary a year ago.

Whenever one of them had a trip planned the other two got as excited as if they were themselves getting to take the trip. And when the traveler would return, she would have brought back small souvenirs for the other two and they would get together to drink coffee, hear about the trip and dream about the three of them going to Europe together. Though none of them realistically thought it would ever happen they delighted in the very prospect of it nonetheless.

They were three best friends who needed and supported each other. They each knew that no one understood her like the other two when it came to what they worried about or what made them feel sad. Each of them seemed to do her fair share of worrying over kids or grand kids or husbands and they all took their turn at feeling low. And then they would worry about each other. Which explains why when one of them was in trouble, the other two deployed to rescue. Around the upstairs table they would gather with a pot of the best pour over coffee in Lakeview. And the best part was that it almost always helped and that there was always laughter. It was the girlfriend fix that they all needed so they were driven to protect it.

But unfortunately even after a pot of pour over and some tears, neither of them had been able to help Clarys this time. And she had left uncharacteristically early to go home and do laundry causing Carmen and Isabelle to raise their eyebrows at each other across the table as Clarys stood up to leave. What was worse was that they were going into a weekend and wouldn't be able to check on Clarys until Monday. "Something is wrong ," Carmen said. "I'll send her a text and see how she's' doing tonight". But they parted for the weekend feeling worried and afraid that this time something was really wrong.

Chapter 16

Clarys seemed to manage to get her spirits up on her own which wasn't unusual for any of the three friends. It hadn't been that long ago when Clarys and Isabelle had been worried for Carmen. Carmen was Latin. Her parents had immigrated to the Unites States from Spain then settled in California where they raised Carmen and her sister. Years later, Carmen met her sailor who was an Iowa farmer and she came home with him to northern Iowa where she had been cold ever since. But even though she was always cold, Carmen was hot even at 60. She was hot natured, hot tempered, and hot to look at. With her Latin ancestry it was no surprise that Carmen was emotionally passionate. Isabelle found herself sympathetic to Carmen's outburst because Isabelle just found it validating to see someone else besides herself pitch a fit over something. How she wished Carmen was more out-spoken about her politics. She could be a force to reckon with but she held her politics close and avoided political discussions except when you got her ire up.

And could Carmen ever pitch a fit if you pushed the right button! She was thought by some, which very possibly might even include her family members, to have a hair trigger. Isabelle had heard someone say once about Carmen, "She's scary!" Carmen had opinions for sure and she freely expressed them not always waiting for an invitation before doing so. She could over-talk anyone she disagreed with and out-pace them in how fast she talked. Isabelle didn't always think Carmen was listening. Not even when she texted her. She once texted her to ask when she would be home and Carmen's response was "I'm in Vegas". Duh, thought Isabelle as she swiped her response "that's what I mean." One of the most amusing things Carmen ever said to Isabelle was that she didn't argue. She literally thought she walked away from arguments and though Isabelle could have countered that statement, she really didn't want to argue with Carmen. She would have lost to Carmen in an argument with her defending her statement that she didn't argue! Though she may have lacked internal truthfulness seeing things as she wanted them to be and not as they were, Carmen had an abundance of passion, emotions, and opinions, and everyone knew not to cross her when it came to her children. Though she could be a like a momma grizzly, scary she wasn't. Not at least as far as Clarys and Isabelle were concerned.

They saw past the temper, the rage, and the outbursts. They saw more complexity to Carmen than most people did. What they saw was a friend who was a mother and grandmother. Though they would admit their friend could sometimes be completely irrational and blinded by her own rage, they insisted that the engine that drove that passion was always and forever her love for her kids and grandkids. Carmen was known for being able to spew forth verbal venom making you feel like your eyes had just been scratched out. She could be a momma pit bull. But almost always if you got to the bottom of it, she was unapologetically, unrequitedly, and undeniably protecting her babies. And that made all the difference to Isabelle. Even if she wasn't always right, and her friends knew she wasn't, she wouldn't back down when it came to those kids and that was something Isabelle and Clarys not only understood but respected Carmen for. In truth Isabelle had never really seen Carmen in her full court press. But she believed it. The thing was that for Isabelle and Clarys there was another Carmen whose passion they had witnessed in her non-rage meltdowns. They had seen Carmen cry. They had seen her vulnerability and her caring. They knew that passion was not just expressed in her anger, but in her fears and her worries and her helplessness to fix everything that she thought needed fixing for her family.

Carmen was a beautiful mid- 60's dark skinned, dark haired women who stood about 5 feet tall if she wore her wedge sandals. She almost always wore a dress and she was never seen without her make-up. If Isabelle had any doubt that Carmen was a beautiful woman such doubts would have been crushed the day her own grandkids had told Isabelle that they thought Poppa needed a girlfriend. It was while Isabelle was away from Henry for two weeks waiting for her daughter to have a baby and she had asked the kids if they thought their poppa was missing her.

"Poppa needs a girlfriend", one of them said.

"Do you think so? But, I am Poppa's girlfriend," Isabelle had replied.

"No, Carmen should be his girlfriend. She's pretty and younger than you," they had replied. To which Isabelle had no response other than that Carmen's hair was not natural and she was in fact older!

Carmen was as frugal as she was beautiful. She might deny herself something but she would never deny her family anything they asked of her. So when on his deathbed she promised her father that she would not forget her cousins in Spain, Carmen made a life commitment that she would travel to Spain every few years to honor her parents and keep that promise. And she had honored that promise several times since her father's passing even taking her children and grandchildren with her. Which brought Isabelle and Clarys to why they had been worried for her recently.

Carmen had let herself get a year overdue making her bi-annual trip to visit her cousins. But at last the passports, flight tickets, car rental and hotel reservations were all made and Carmen was counting down to the day she would leave. The problem was that this time she was going to have to leave behind one of her daughters and three of her grandkids and it was causing her no end of distress. "What can we do for her?" Clarys and Isabelle were asking each other. And of course the answer was, " Let's get her to come upstairs for some coffee."

It wasn't easy to get Carmen to stop for coffee. She was the one of the three of them who always had a grandchild with a birthday, a daughter needing help with child care, work, or just helping her single-parent daughter and her three kids in Lakeview. Layer on that, the fact that Carmen's husband was a farmer and she would help with planting and harvest during certain months of the year and it made her busier than Clarys and Isabelle put together! Three of Carmen's grandkids lived in Lakeview and she liked to attend their school events and because she *could* get to the out of town grandkids in just a two hour drive, she tried to keep it fair by going to their programs, games, and special events too.

Even though Clary's and Isabelle had tried to get Carmen to go out to lunch with them or have a girls day of shopping, the best they could hope for, they had learned, was coffee upstairs. And even that was a long shot. But once in awhile Carmen would just put up a closed sign at work and announce she was coming upstairs for coffee. Isabelle would text Clarys and Clarys would drop everything and walk from her apartment. Isabelle would get the cups warm, grind the coffee, and heat the pot to make a round of pour-over. The aroma of the grinding Italian City Roast would drift down the hall and stairs and greet Clarys and Carmen when they opened the door. Sometimes there would be coffee cake or cookies under the glass dome on the big table but if not, Isabelle would go to her chocolate stash to share some 85% cacao to have with their coffee. It would always be to Isabelle's great delight that Clarys would take her first sip and then close her eyes, and whisper, "That is so good!"

"Are you excited?" Clarys and Isabelle asked Carmen immediately. It turned out to be a difficult question for Carmen to answer. What emerged was a mix of emotions ranging from worry over the ones she was leaving behind, to sadness over the cousins who have passed since her last visit, to sadness over the cousins she will see for the last time and not even knowing who they are, to her excitement over returning to her parent's family members and their homes but saddened to return with only her memories of them to take with her. Yes, Carmen was in full Latin mode, juggling about eight emotions at the same time and she needed to melt down before she left. Carmen needed to feel the support of her friends and the table they sat around. She needed to lay it all out, right there, on that table before she left for Spain. She needed to leave a little less burdened, a little less regretful, and a little less sad. And so listening was what Isabelle and Clarys did to get her there. And when the cups were cold and the chocolate was gone and the hours had passed, Carmen had laid her worries down on that table and there were hugs all around, bon voyages said, and promises made. Carmen promised to instagram everything. Isabelle and Clarys promised to be there for Mary and the kids and check on them everyday. And the three friends parted agreeing once again that it would be such fun if they could all take a trip to Spain together someday, knowing it was never going to happen.

Chapter 17

Isabelle was riding along in the car deep in thought. Henry was listening to the radio on their drive across Iowa after a weekend trip. Isabelle stared out the window at the rows of maturing corn. The sky was blue. The air was absolutely still. Not a weed was moving. The crops looked parched with thirst waiting for the sun to go down so they could drink in the cool night air. The sun was bright and it was hot. The last few days had been brutally hot which Isabelle enjoyed.

Isabelle was ready to get home. She loved weekends away but ever since she opened upstairs she found herself ready to go home and go back to her coffee shop. There was just something about it that gave Isabelle a sense of purpose and peace. She felt balanced and grounded when she was upstairs.

It was the people, she knew. Isabelle had figured out that humans, at least most humans, need to be around other people. She had only recently figured it out during a visit to her elderly mother and ever since then she felt she better understood herself and rural populations and why she felt so isolated on their acreage and in the community in general.

Isabelle's mother was in Isabelle's words, "a piece of work". She was a miserably unhappy 84 year old woman who was fixated on everything she didn't have. She was lonely, bitter, and increasingly manipulative. She spent 90 % of her time alone. She rarely interacted with other people. She might have been distracted by some socializing if she hadn't insisted on living in a house on a cul de sac in a neighborhood where everyone was at work all day. But at 75 she had bought herself a ranch style house reminiscent of the one she had raised her family in and none of the six kids had had the chutzpah to refuse to let her do it.

It wasn't like she had been a good candidate for aging gracefully. Sadly she had been raised in the south and had no education beyond 8th grade. A beautiful woman when she was younger, Isabelle's mother had married a man who Isabelle suspected had wanted a trophy wife. Her father would describe Isabelle's mother as having had a coke bottle figure in her youth. She also had a thick head of auburn hair and legs to die for.

Isabelle's dad was GI Bill educated. Also raised in the south, he had attended pharmacy school and done well in business after getting out of the Navy. Both of her parents were lacking in social graces, polish and refinement but her dad at least was pretty well read. In their world in a small Kansas town they were big fish in a little pond hobnobbing with the "better to do". They had worked hard, saved and budgeted their money well allowing them to occasionally play hard as well escaping to Kansas City Playboy night clubs, New York City Broadway shows, and enjoying material comforts and post industrial era wealth.

Sadly Isabelle's father had died in his late 60's leaving her mother angry, alone, and feeling cheated. With an adolescent mind in many ways, even though she had done a great job of raising six kids, Isabelle's mother had spent the last 30 years feeling sorrier and sorrier for herself making it difficult for Isabelle to have any relationship at all with her.

There were many explanations for why she was who she was and why Isabelle and she didn't have a close relationship and Isabelle had spent many hours in self therapy and with Henry and friends trying to figure it all out. But nothing, she had

concluded, did she believe with more conviction

than that for at least the last 10 years of her life her

mother had been starved for more socialization.

And that was a lesson Isabelle intended to learn

from. It was why she was beginning to better

understand her own restlessness and it was going to

inform her future decisions.

Isabelle's mother, in her own misery, had

inadvertently given Isabelle the gift of identifying

what it was that gave her a rush from being around

people, even if you didn't know them. It was from

observing her mother's unhappiness made Isabelle

come to understand her own yearning to live in a

bigger more vibrant place where she would be near

coffee shops, book shops, parks, walking trails and

neighborhoods. Upstairs had been a tiny dose, at

long last, to that yearning and she was ready to go

home and be with her people.

But regarding her future and decisions about it, Isabelle was feeling out of control lately. Isabelle had known for the last month that her job of 16 years was going to be changing and changing dramatically. The florists could no longer afford her contract fee and they were reviewing everything about her job and expecting to make some "adjustments" to her contract. If she was reading between the lines right, what Isabelle knew was that she might lose her job but at the very least she would not have the same job. And lately she had grown more and more concerned that they just might decide not to renew her contract at all.

Not only were there concerns about her job security but she was feeling undervalued and disrespected by the people with whom she worked most closely. Isabelle had loved her job for 16 years and she was convinced that her members had respected her. But the new leadership was feeling like a coup and Isabelle was feeling distrusted and rejected. She was beginning to wonder not only if her job was ending but more importantly if she even wanted it anymore.

Suddenly Isabelle blurted out "I feel like I'm losing my identity, Henry", and her voice broke.

"Yes, I can imagine", Henry responded.

"My job is part of who I am. People have looked up to me and respected me. If I don't have my job I'm just going to be viewed as a grandma. Grandmas aren't respected in our culture. You don't count if you're just a grandma. No one cares what you think or considers you even relevant. I love being a Grandma, Henry, but I want to be seen as more than that."

"Well it's not completely true that Grandmas aren't respected Isabelle" Henry said. "But I know what you're saying,"

"It's just that I hadn't thought about that until now. I've been worried about what I would do with myself. And I'm worried about losing the coffee shop. I've thought about all the things I could do. I could play the piano more. I could read more. I could knit more. I could start sewing again and try selling stuff on Etsy. But EVERY SINGLE ONE OF THOSE THINGS IS DONE IN ISOLATION. I NEED SOCIAL INTERACTION, HENRY!" and with that, the tears began to flow.

"I hadn't even thought about losing my identity and now I think that will be the worst part".

Henry felt terrible for Isabelle but there was nothing he could say. He knew she was right. He knew that the hardest part about retiring would probably be the loss of purpose and relevance. He had begun to recognize that himself as he observed people around him retiring. Henry was himself figuring out how to know when he should retire and what to do when he did. They both knew that they couldn't watch game shows, sit in lawn chairs on the Arizona desert for two months in the winter, or drink coffee every morning in a Lakeview right wing echo chamber of senior citizens. Thye rode along in silence.

Isabelle had been mulling over in her mind how she could reinvent herself, if she lost her job, for the past several weeks.. Her first and most immediate concern had been that she might lose the coffee shop. But she hoped that even if she had no income she would be able to keep the coffee shop open just so she had *something* to do. But then she realized that the only reason the coffee shop worked for her was because she had her job to keep her busy during those hours when there was no one in the shop. And to be honest there were plenty of days when hardly anyone came in, though there had never been a day since she opened it that at least 1 person hadn't come in for coffee. But she knew that the days could get just as long upstairs as they did at home if all she did was read or knit. She knew she would need more. *"But from where? How? Where do I fit into my own future?"* she wondered.

"This isn't going to be as easy as closing the studio, you know, Henry. When I did that I replaced it with the coffee shop. But this job uses up way more time in my day than the studio every did!" said Isabelle.

"Well I wish I had an answer. You are over-qualified for most jobs in Stone County and that's a problem. No one wants to move someplace they can't find a job. Lakeview hospital might be able to recruit a doctor but what will her husband do if he's a chemical engineer or something? That doesn't help, I know. It's just a factor of the obsolescence of rural areas."

Pulling in the driveway, Isabelle put her thoughts aside and helped Henry unload the car. They had plenty to do for the next hour watering pots of flowers, getting the mail, emptying their suitcases, and starting laundry. It was already late and they wanted to start out the next morning caught up before they left for work.

Clarys had texted Isabelle to see if they could have coffee at eight o'clock the next morning before she left for the rest of the week. Isabelle wanted to make sure that happened. So after completing all her domestic tasks she spent what was left of the evening going through office mail, checking messages, organizing her brief case, and figuring out what to take for lunch the next morning that would be a quick pack. By 9:30 Isabelle had finished her glass of wine, heard the best half of the late broadcast of the news hour, and was heading up to bed. I'll worry about things tomorrow she told herself in her best internal Scarlet O'Hara voice. Then, exhausted from the weekend, she soon was fast asleep.

The next morning dawned bright and hot again. At 6:30 it was already 78 degrees. The heat index was to be at 115 degrees by midday and the radio announcements were cautioning listeners to stay hydrated and in air conditioning. Henry was already in the kitchen sending up aromas of sautéing garlic and freshly ground coffee when Isabelle was slipping into her blue and white seersucker sun dress. For once Isabelle didn't agonize over what to wear. Stepping into her birkenstocks she headed down the stairs for her espresso.

By 7:30 she was in her car having already made
their lunches and gone all around the house pulling
shades and shutting windows that had collected the
cool night air. She pointed her car southward and
began her drive toward Lakeview listening to NPR
as she drove. She pulled up to the curb in front of
the coffee shop by 7:45. As soon as she had opened
the coffee shop, she texted Clarys that she was
ready for coffee and was in the kitchen filtering
cold press when she heard the glass door bang shut
at the bottom of the stairs signaling to her that
Clarys had arrived.

Seeing Clarys walk into the shop already wiping her
brow, Isabelle knew she better re-set the thermostat.
Today was not the day to keep upstairs at 78
degrees. Isabelle sat down with her iced coffee.
Clarys went to the coffee bar to make her pour over

to take on her road trip. In just the few minutes she took to make her coffee Clarys had picked up on Isabelle's mood. It wasn't hard. Isabelle was never glum or down. But clearly something was different today. "What's up?" Clarys asked sitting down at the table.

With only a short ½ hour before Clarys had to hit the road, Isabelle kept it short not reiterating the litany of grievances she had expressed to Henry the day before. She figured they could talk when Clarys was back next week but now was not the time. There just wasn't time. She needed to talk to Clarys but it was going to have to wait. As it turned out, Isabelle and Clarys wouldn't see each other again for a month, by which time Isabelle thought she had moved closer to accepting the inevitable changes in her life.

Chapter 18

Summer was waning and there was finally welcome relief from the heat. The air was already getting a little cooler and crisper. Mornings were feeling more like fall and Isabelle was restless bored. It seemed like everyone and their brother was doing something fun, going places, and posting pictures of their awesome lives on their facebook pages. Isabelle was complaining to Henry that their lives were stagnant and lacking in vibrancy and excitement. Vacation for her and Henry was still over a month away. The prospect of nothing out of the ordinary in her immediate future was unacceptable. So one morning, she sent an email message, subject line "smooches and hugs", to her oldest daughter Andy, mother of her three grandkids. "In need of a fix," her message said.

"When is a good time for me to come up?" "*Let's put this potential retirement status to the test,*" thought Isabelle. "*Impulse will be the name of the game for me from now on if things turn out like I'm expecting.*"

The text message worked. Two days later Isabelle was on her way to Minneapolis. She adored her three grandkids and though she knew she couldn't (and didn't want to) move in with them, it was one of her greatest delights to spend a few days in the cities where she could walk one of the girls to her school by the Dunn Brother's coffee shop and stroll the youngest around the downtown lake where they would stop near the bandshell and have a glass of ice cold lemonade. She loved her time there and the thought passed through her mind that doing more of this in the future, depending on how her job turned out, might just be okay.

Some of the time she was there, Isabelle had time to herself while the kids were at school, the youngest was with the nanny and the two parents were working. That was when she would set out on foot for what she called her urban hikes. She would put on her boots, maybe a hat if it was cool, wrap her neck in a bright scarf, and with her back pack of essentials on her back she would just go out and roam around the neighborhoods.

Isabelle had always been great at pretending which is where her mind would go on her flaneuring through the neighborhoods imagining that she would someday live in one of the them. She would look carefully at each house and pretend it was hers. She would establish in her wanderings that her "must haves" would include an enclosed porch, breakfast nook, and a fireplace. She would automatically dismiss corner lots because of snow removal responsibilities and would give

consideration to living on a busy street as long as

she had an alley entrance for her car and a backdoor

that would be her exit ramp to the walk-able

neighborhoods. When her feet were tired she would

find a coffee shop or a park bench. Sometimes, if

she had remembered to bring it along, she would

take pictures with her old studio camera. It had

always been urban photography that she had liked

the best.

For years Isabelle had created photo albums of

urban themed art she just saved in her computer.

One was called "Working Men" and included shots

from Washington DC to San Francisco, from street

level road construction crews to 30 story high

window washers from the window of her hotel

room. Another album was just pictures of street

murals and graffiti. She had a few favorite murals

from Santiago Chile one of which she had spent extra money to have giclee printed onto stretched canvas. A less favorite, but one of her oldest albums, was her lampposts album. She had been on that kick during a weekend in Chicago and had especially enjoyed the Oak Park neighborhood walk for that series. And of course, there were her row house pictures and the beautiful colors in the hill side pictures she had taken in Valparaiso Chile. Isabelle especially liked the colors of the blocks of row houses in DC. The immaculate landscaping and property maintenance drew her in and she could imagine her and Henry living in a row house and departing in the morning to the busy sidewalk at the bottom of their steps where they would walk to a coffee shop and read the New York Times. *"Oh, if only ..."* Isabelle would think. But *"if only what?"* her inner voice would respond.

If he wasn't with her, Isabelle always missed Henry and after two days she was usually ready to head back home. This time when she was heading back to Henry, she had an extra day to stop by their cabin in the north woods and check that everything had been left intact from their last guests.

As much as she had time alone at home, there was nothing quite like time alone at the cabin. It wasn't that she did anything all that different than she did at home. It was just that it was totally away from Lakview and it was absolutely solitary.

A cabin had been Isabelle's idea. She had imagined a cabin in the mountains or isolated in a north woods forest on a lake. The cabin they got was nothing even close to that, but it was as close as she was ever going to get and she knew it. So when Henry found them a 600 square foot fishing shack on a lake in a developed area with neighbors on both sides northwest of the twin cities, they bought it. It was the same week they had taken Ivy, the fourth of their four daughters to college. Isabelle would tell the story that she and Henry went home. They looked at each other. They could have heard a pin drop. Isabelle would say she had whispered, "Are they all gone?" to which Henry had said, "I think so".

"Is there any money left?" Isabelle pretended having asked.

Then, she would say, "We counted our money and screamed let's go buy a cabin!"

Isabelle was as happy as a clam. The first time they were in their cabin after they closed the deal, they popped open the bottle of wine they had brought back from Montepulciano Italy and which they had saved for just such a special occasion. Ever since then that bottle had sat on the cabin kitchen table with a taper candle in it.

Henry had chosen their cabin because of its location relative to Minneapolis. It was close to the North Star commuter train and if he didn't miss his guess it was in a growth area. Growth meant property value increases and property value increases meant good investment and good investments always meant money. So even though it was a pretty far cry from her dream cabin, with Henry's talent and hard work the fishing shack had eventually been transformed to the cutest little Minnesota lake cabin anyone would want. And they both loved it.

At the cabin alone, Isabelle would sleep when she wanted to, eat what she wanted to, and read as much as she wanted to. She would lay in her hammock under the giant oak trees and gaze endlessly at the sky day dreaming and watching the squirrels fly between the branches in the canopy of trees, chasing and scolding each other until she would fall asleep. If she had to go to the store she would, but if she could avoid leaving the cabin she would rummage around for almost anything to eat and stay right there. It was her little piece of paradise and she longed to be closer and go more often.

Part of its charm was that the cabin had a sloping knotty pine ceiling in the kitchen. On the bedroom wall Isabelle had made a collage hanging black and white pictures of friends and family members. Scattered throughout the three rooms were homemade shelves Henry had made each of the girls for their rooms when they still lived at home. On those shelves were short story books, movies for the kids, Minnesota ghost story books and pieces of memorabilia from home that never had quite the right place in that house but seemed to just belong at the cabin. On one wall they had hung a pair of old snow shoes, Isabelle's dad's cross country skis, and a row of hooks on which Isabelle had hung her mom's red wool Filson jacket her dad had bought her when they were younger. For a cabin they hadn't owned all that long, it was full of memories and souvenirs from random places that all contributed to make it feel very familiar and cozy and they loved spending time there.

Normally when she was there by herself two days was enough, but this time, even though she would have liked another day there, Isabelle had only one night as she had planned to leave the morning after her arrival day. That was okay with Isabelle since she knew the new norm might include a lot of days alone at the cabin in her future.

The next morning, Isabelle woke to the distant call of the loon and jumping out of bed, skipping her coffee, she was on the lake in her kayak before the sun was up. It was a calm warm morning and in spite of the repellent and her straw sun hat, the mosquitoes were swarming her so badly that Isabelle cut short her kayaking to head back and make her espresso. The sky turned cloudy and the temps began to drop by mid-morning when Isabelle decided she might as well just go home. She packed up, planning to lolly-gag her way home stopping often and maybe stopping at the Rock Rapids coffee shop where she could connect to the internet and catch up on her email or read a little. There was no reason to hurry home. *"Henry wouldn't be home until 5:00 or after anyway. It's time to slow down and enjoy the moments, right?"* thought Isabelle. Taking it slow and leisurely was the plan. Isabelle turned off the power to the pump, made sure the stove was off, checked that all of the ceiling fans were off, made sure she had her phone and her charger and then locking the cabin door behind her she got in her car. But she was no more out of the cabin driveway when her phone chimed. "I think I'll feel like coffee this afternoon", she read in a post by Harmony on the upstairs facebook page.

Isabelle knew that was code for "I am hoping someone else wants coffee this afternoon and will meet me there." And in that moment, Isabelle changed her plans about driving slow and being all leisurely on her way home. That text made her decide to head right to the upstairs coffee shop instead. With her plan to dilly dally her way home scrapped, Isabelle set off on her four hour drive looking forward to some time with at least Harmony and maybe others.

While she had been gone, the week in politics had been tumultuous and she had missed it all with no one to talk to about it. Arriving upstairs by two o'clock later that afternoon, smelling the coffee beans as she opened the door at the bottom of the stairs, Isabelle was glad she was back.

As she ascended the stairs Isabelle heard voices and was surprised but pleased to find Lars and another member visiting over coffee.

"Where's Harmony?" she asked.

"No idea," Lars said.

"She said she was coming this afternoon. I figured she was here when I heard you, but it is a little early for her. She usually comes a little later in the afternoon."

"Text her and tell her to come now", Lars said.

Which Isabelle did. And to which Harmony responded "Let me get my civies on." Which meant she was leaving her collar at home. It made Isabelle giggle inside to think of Harmony as a regular person.

By mid afternoon the table was full and lively with five members talking about everything from the DNC, to food insecurities, to sexism … which may have been why Lars left! Isabelle had made the right decision to head home without delay.

Navigating retirement, if indeed retirement was to be her new status, would mean discovering, she decided. It would be about engagement with others wherever she could find it. It would be about discovering the simple pleasures and discovering the richness you found surrounding you. It would be about moments just like this. The satisfaction from the laughter, the occasional profanity and the great coffee was just what the doctor had ordered for Isabelle. She locked up to head home to Henry and the News Hour feeling satisfied and knowing that

she had come home to her happy place. Both of

them.

Chapter 19

After her too short visit to her north woods cabin, Isabelle had hoped that she would be able to still get away for another couple of days alone at the cabin, but September came and went. And then October. And by mid-November it still hadn't happened and by then it was time to antifreeze the drains, blow out water pipes, and leave it for the harsh cold blasts of the north woods. There would be no going back alone until next year. The disappointment of never getting back might have been more upsetting but for the cloud of despair that hung over Isabelle after the November election.

Isabelle and Clarys had spent much of late summer and fall working again on the campaign for Hillary Clinton. Though neither of them was as energized initially as they had been for the primaries, they bucked it up for the cause and spent hours door knocking again, this time to "get out the vote" in Lakeview in October and even traveling on election day to knock doors in the packing plant town 35 miles west of them where 18 different languages were spoken by the citizenry that included large populations of Laotians, Sudanese, Somalians and Hispanics. They were super pumped on election day as they met at the coffee shop in their pantsuits to suck down there shots of espresso and spend what was a beautiful fall day hitting the sidewalk to knock doors, chat up potential voters and advance the agenda of the campaign.

They left by eight o'clock in the morning in Isabelle's car and 45 minutes later found the campaign headquarters in a private home in a residential section of town. Isabelle pulled up to the curb and double checked the address. There were no signs marking the house as a political office of any sort but the address she got in her email from the field representative was exactly where Google maps had routed them. Somewhat hesitatingly, they went up on the porch together and knocked on the door. A man answered the door and invited them in.

The house was clearly a residence but the front room had been converted to a campaign headquarters. There were signs, buttons, clipboards, and several pamphlets in neat stacks on a six foot church table in the owner's living room. Bottles of water were sitting on the floor and a basket of red, white and blue DNC pens was at the end of table. The furniture in the room had all been pushed back to make room for the campaign table but the family pictures, or rather portraits, hanging on the walls spoke to the relative wealth of the people who lived there.

Isabelle identified herself and Clarys to the man who had greeted them thinking he would offer them water, hand them a clipboard of addresses and send them off. But she was soon to find out that was not the protocol. Apparently his job was to train the female volunteers as they showed up to get their materials. It was clear to Isabelle and Clarys as he mansplained how to knock on a door, read a script and mark a form that his job was "management' and theirs was entry level. As far as Isabelle had been able to tell in her many times of volunteering over the years, men only got involved if they were paid, fed, or made to feel in charge.

Isabelle was not a patient person. Nor was she a rude person. But in that moment she was becoming a fed up person. It there was one thing this campaign had uncovered it was the strength and conviction of women who had too long felt like second class citizens to a male dominated society. As the man delivered his condescending script of instructions, repeating them to make sure the simple minded women were comprehending them, Isabelle and Clarys proceeded to move towards the door to depart on their terms refusing to take orders from a man who had probably never door knocked for a candidate in hisl life.

"Well that felt good", said Isabelle. "I hate to be rude but I believe that man was offending me! Did anyone mention to him that we are volunteers? Not to mention competent and experienced door knockers!"

 Energized by the reminder of why they were doing this, Isabelle was as fearless as she had ever been. She and Clarys were determined to knock every door they were assigned. They were ready to face down the squalor of long hallways in run down apartment buildings or go inside trailer houses that looked like they that might have been meth labs. Isabelle was eager to use her limited Spanish skills if necessary and was hoping she would get the chance. They were happy to support the Mexican bakery and drink the bad coffee just to let the owners know what they were doing and encourage them to vote and get their community out to vote as well. The stakes were high but the polls had been favorable and though they both harbored tiny seeds of doubt, the day was planned to end in a victory celebration.

Returning to Lakeview by mid afternoon dehydrated, with blistered feet, famished and still pumping adrenalin, Isabelle departed Clarys planning to meet up later for an election returns wine event at the coffee shop. It wasn't out of the ordinary to flip the coffee shop to a wine bar for special events and this was an event that certainly merited such a flip.

Scheduled to start at four o'clock that afternoon, the air was electric upstairs as members started showing up a half hour early, dropping in and out, and speculating with each other about the what ifs that would follow if their candidates lost. Isabelle opened a bottle of merlot and some chardonnay. Members brought in party mix, pizza, jars of olives, pickles, cheese, sausage, and someone even brought pickled herring knowing Henry would be there.

The planned two hour event was still in progress three hours later at seven o'clock. And at eight o'clock the energy and excitement was palpable. Two more bottles of wine had been opened as some 15 members of both genders, both young and old, had shown up for the event. Everyone was excited.

No one wanted to leave. But with plans to join Henry and Clarys at Clarys' house to watch the returns, Isabelle finally just announced she was leaving and left upstairs a little after eight with members still enjoying wine.

"Just leave the mess and whoever leaves last can lock the door with the magnet key and stick it under my bicycle seat when you leave," Isabelle said. Later that night it would turn out that Isabelle would wish they had all stayed a little longer to enjoy themselves while they still could. It turned out that while they were drinking their wine the election had already started going go south. It was only an hour after they met up at Clarys' when reality hit.

The living room in Clarys' house was deadpan silent as the three of them watched the election returns in disbelief. They were shocked to see their candidate slowly losing electoral votes in state after state that had not even been in question. The pundits were reporting with disbelief as live election statisticians were crunching numbers, projecting, analyzing and trying to make sense of what was happening for the viewers as it was unfolding right before their eyes. The night was going to be long for the networks and the results were going to be close. Americans would go to bed not knowing for sure who their next president would be. Finally by ten o'clock that night Isabelle and Henry left a somber Clarys to head home thanking her for her hospitality and promising to meet upstairs the next day.

Like most of the rest of America, Isabelle had a sleepless night watching the clock pass every hour. Having gone to bed at ten thirty and then checking returns a little before midnight, she finally went to sleep knowing that Hillary still had a chance but it didn't look good for her, and she would just have to wait until morning.

 By five o'clock the next morning, she could no longer resist and Isabelle opened her phone to learn the devastating news that Hillary Clinton, the first female candidate of a major party, the woman who had more qualifications than any presidential candidate in history, the woman who was to have finally crashed through the glass ceiling sending the message to the world that in America any young girl could dream to be president one day … had lost.

 It would be weeks before the world would know that she had won the popular vote. And it would be more weeks before the world would know for sure that Russia had intervened in the U.S. Election to tip the scales that handed the presidency to the narcissistic republican nominee Donald Trump, a man known to have sexually assaulted and insulted women with no shame or remorse. But none of that was known or mattered, yet. The reality of the now and what that meant to America and America's women was the raw reality that had to be faced.

Isabelle put her phone down and lay in bed and sobbed. She couldn't believe it. She was in shock. She couldn't sort the myriad of thoughts converging in her mind. She was angry that a racist, misogynistic, Islamophobic, bully had won the election. She thought of her four daughters and her two granddaughters. She thought of all the women who had been denied opportunities and equality because of their gender. Her mother who never even knew how oppressed she was. Herself for never having held herself to her highest potential because she had never even had the imagination to dream of being more than what had been identified to her as her choices and of having only realized while raising her own daughters how short she had sold herself. She thought of her four daughters who had aspired to achieve and had succeeded but were still facing hurdles in the workplace for pay and equal treatment. She thought of her granddaughters for whom she had so much hope. Hillary Clinton had symbolized for Isabelle all that she could have aspired to and didn't. She saw Hillary as the champion who was going to fight for more gender equity in the workplace and for more rights for women and children where Isabelle herself had invested her own life.

Isabelle had always been about raising empowered daughters and believing in families and children. She had held Hillary out as a hero for all women and all generations of women. Hillary was to have opened the door for all to come after and she had carried the burden for all who had come before. She had been the professional who was also a mom and who supported all women no matter the choices they had made for themselves that had differed from hers. Hillary was the woman who wasn't threatened by the choices, mistakes or even the politics of other women. She spoke and fought for all of them and she had spent her life doing it. Isabelle thought of all these things and more and she sobbed uncontrollably.

By eight o'clock Isabelle was at the coffee shop. She hadn't put on makeup because she knew she was not going to be able to stop crying. She only had a few hours before she would be leaving for Minneapolis but she needed to see her friends Clarys and Carmen before she left. As comforting as her husband Henry was, and he too was disappointed in the election, Isabelle needed the comfort of other women at least for a few hours before she left for the rest of the week. Only they

could understand truly the despair she was feeling.

Chapter 20

The upstairs was like a morgue the morning after
the election. Thankfully someone had cleaned up
from the party. There was disbelief, devastation,
and anger. Hugs, tears and consolations were shared
but there was little anyone could really say that was
going to make a difference. It was clear it was going
to take more than a day to get over this
disappointment. It would turn out that it would take
weeks and months. It would turn out to impact all of
America and the members of upstairs in deeply
personal ways not even yet expected.

Isabelle left that morning for her daughter Andy's
house in Minneapolis. Driving alone for over three
hours with the radio on, hearing the pundits
expressions of disbelief and their attempts at some

analysis, bawling her way through the concession speech, and blowing her nose as she drove, Isabelle was able to get it together by the time she reached her daughter's house where she was to babysit for the rest of the week.

For Isabelle the grieving over the loss of the election ended up having to be put on hold. Arriving in Minneapolis after her tearful drive, she picked up her grandchildren discovering that the youngest had become very sick in the few hours since Andy and her husband had flown out that morning. Isabelle spent the next 5 days just trying to get through caring for three children. She would find herself doing what she had done for 30 years. She became consumed with getting meals on the table, kids to bed, laundry done, swimming lessons, piano lessons, lunches packed, and finally getting them out the door to school in time to not miss the bus.

But most importantly, Isabelle was consumed with worrying over and cuddling a very fussy feverish baby. Here she was again doing the traditional work of a mother or grandmother. Though she was very happy to be doing it, it wasn't lost on her that fate might be reminding her of her place in the grand scheme of things as a woman. Had she dwelled on it she might have sunk into a deeper despair. But there was no time or energy to spend thinking of herself. Sleep deprived, Isabelle was giving all of her energy to the care of the children. So a week later when she returned to the coffee shop having emotionally fast tracked and already having decided to become a local social activist, she was met with friends still in anger mode and the upstairs mood still dark and hopeless.

 Listening to a couple of members a few days later talk about workplace discrimination they had experienced, Isabelle began to second guess herself and feel like an outsider to an elite club. She had not experienced workplace discrimination and sexism like Clarys and some of the other women had who shared their stories. While they were trying to be family providers in a patriarchal society, Isabelle had been consumed with just what had occupied her the first week after the election. She had spent her life being a mother and homemaker. Hearing them vent and share their stories with each other left Isabelle feeling a little lonely, invalidated and undeserving of even joining the conversation.

Sometimes Isabelle felt like she had been sheltered. While Clarys, Connie and others had been on the front lines fighting for equality in the workplace and suffering sexual discrimination, Isabelle had been home raising her family, insulated and even unaware of the oppression her sisters in the work world were dealing with. To be fair, she had been grooming daughters to believe in their own ability to break glass ceilings. Which was why, ultimately Isabelle believed she had a stake in the movement too. Tempted to chastise herself for presuming entitlement to participate in the outrage, Isabelle instead gifted herself the right to sound her voice with no apologies for the choices she had made .

"So you damn right," she thought. *"now when the ultimate breakthrough has been so close, the breakthrough that was going to make life easier for my daughters to advance their own careers, this defeat is just as personal for me as it is for my sisters who were in the trenches facing down the patriarchy. We're all sisters here even though I never made it into the trenches. I would have if the stars had aligned differently!"*

The election had changed the upstairs coffee shop.

For their own reasons, a couple of members went

AWOL. One in particular, Christy, confessed that

she had not been able to return until she had

recovered from the dramatic emotional plunge

between the election night wine event and the next

morning's news. Christy had also been dealing with

the reality that her husband had voted for Trump.

Another member never did talk about her absence

but her visits after the election were fewer and

farther apart. Isabelle was worried that members

had felt a political vibe they couldn't endorse and

though that made Isabelle sad, she also knew that

her private coffee shop was, and needed to be, a

place for the community of liberal political outcasts.

The liberal leaning members of upstairs who felt

like they were in the political margins of the

community had no other place to gather. It wasn't

even easy for them to find each other in the larger

community. Upstairs had found its voice and its place with them. And Isabelle was not inclined to apologize for that.

A few weeks after the election, Isabelle and Clarys treated themselves to some road trip therapy that helped get their mind off their disappointment. A trip to Des Moines for coffee, Italian food, and walking around East Village turned out to be therapeutic and they both returned to Lakeview in a better place mentally and emotionally. And even though they wanted to keep a little anger alive and remain energized for change, Isabelle was ready to think about the holidays and feel happy again. She needed a break. It was exhausting to stay angry. It had been exhausting to cry so much. They had sought solace and found it. Time was healing their wounds. But it was not erasing them. Complacency was not going to root in. The salve that had soothed their souls would continue to be engagement in some manner, perhaps just in upstairs discussions, perhaps in activism, or perhaps in something yet to be identified. They needed a break but they would be back. They were done crying for now but they were not going away. They felt purposeful with a tinge of vengeance and that was enough for that moment. As long as they had upstairs, good coffee, and hung onto a little bit of pissiness, they were going to continue to resist and they were going to be okay. Let the holidays begin.

Chapter 21

Isabelle loved Christmas and it was the distraction she was needing. She loved the cooking and the decorating and the memory making. She worked at making Christmas festive and she was good at it. And she had the perfect house for the 7 foot natural balsam fir tree they planned to bring home from the cabin when they went in November.

Isabelle would start Christmas unashamedly early admitting she listened to her Christmas CD's in the car right after Halloween. Anxious to do something festive, in November she invited Sissy and Clarys to come to her house to make butternut squash ravioli and marinated olives.

Isabelle had ordered large restaurant size cans of

Sicilian Olives and Henry had saved back some garden squash in their basement cold storage from the summer harvest to be used for holiday recipes. So one fall night the three of them met in Isabelle's big farm kitchen for an evening to cook, drink wine, roll pasta, and marinate olives and ideas for Christmas.

Isabelle loved her kitchen and never more than when she was cooking with friends or family. It had a large 100 year old oak table in the middle of the room where one could work or around which could be placed at least six chairs. Henry had finally updated the lighting to make every counter space or corner a well lit work station. The perfectly imperfect walls were painted a warm tuscan terracotta. Five black iron skillets in various sizes hung on the wall. In one corner on the counter were mason jars of dried sage, parsley, cilantro, and various other herbs from their own garden. In another corner there were jars of dried beans, rice, orzo, lentils, and a large 2 litre can of olive oil.

 Beside the stove was an old library table that had one drawer that contained more spices and on top of which was a bread box containing nuts, popcorn, and different kinds of dried fruits. Bottles of flavored oils and vinegars and a box of kosher salt and cracked pepper were never put away and sat instead on the top of the bread box where Isabelle could grab what she needed when she was cooking.

It was a kitchen was meant for cooking. In it was a five burner gas stove, five cutting boards, a well supplied drawer of cutlery, and a crock of utensils that sat on the library table with the oils and bread box under the wall of skillets. In that crock a cook could find any kind of spatula, spoon, or strainer she or he might need.

Other people loved Isabelle's kitchen too. Isabelle even thought Julia Child's would have approved of it and had actually tried to organize it in the Julia Child's model. Best of all it was a kitchen where her family had gathered to cook together for over three decades adding in friends and son-in-laws as they joined the family. Just like this night.

The first thing the three friends made were the marinated olives. They stuffed beautiful large Sicilian olives into green mason jars Clarys had brought. They looked ready to wrap up and give as Christmas gifts after the red peppers Isabelle had secured from her daughter Andy, and the lemon wedges, fennel, and coriander seeds were all added. Once the finished jars of olives were admired and set aside they dove into the work of ravioli making.

Isabelle had pre-roasted the squash to a beautiful caramelized brown, before the girls got there, so it would be cooled and ready to mash and mix with butter and cheese for the filling. Setting up an assembly line with Isabelle at the helm they got right to work on the ravioli. Isabelle apologized for her bossiness in assigning tasks but she full well knew that if they were going to be efficient and have anything to show for their time at the end of the night it would be up to her. So while Clary's worked on the filling, Isabelle rolled out the pasta, and Sissy hand-formed the raviolis they shared stories, talked cooking, gossiped a little and sipped their wine.

They talked about missing Carmen wishing she could have joined them and dreamed about planning a dinner with candles and music and courses. They talked about who would come and what to cook and shared their excitement that maybe they could really make it happen. They talked about their own

Holiday traditions. They talked about their families.
They did *not* talk about politics

.By night's end they admitted they were physically
tired but emotionally energized. Each of them ended
up with a gallon bag of partially frozen ravioli,
complimentary fresh sage leaves from Isabelle's
garden for the brown butter sauce they would make
at home, and three pint jars each of the marinated
olives. Clarys and Sissy left, after hugging Isabelle
and thanking her for the memorable night, with a
reminder from Isabelle to watch for deer as they
drove home, and the promise to meet up soon at the
coffee shop.

Cooking and getting together with friends was only
part of Isabelle's enjoyment of the holidays. She
also loved the decorating. Once the fir tree had been
cut and hauled home from Jan's tree farm near her
cabin, Isabelle was ready to decorate the house. It

was Henry's job to help with the tree only until it was standing. After that, his job was to make the eggnog, put on Bing Crosby's White Christmas, and watch Isabelle go through 40 years of decorations selecting her most favorite ones.

"My God, Henry, when did we get so old?" Isabelle asked as she pulled out a glass ball from a fancy satin box. "Look at this one Sammy got us when she studied in Italy. Now this one isn't so old," she said as she held up the little red kayak the girls had gotten them the year they turned 60.

""Where did we get that bird?" Henry asked

"It's a partridge! And Samy got us this one too. It's from P.O.S.H. in Chicago. She knows I love that store and I'm too tight to buy anything there. Now here's an old one! I got this little glass bell from one of the little boys I had in pre-school when we first

moved her. I've hung this on the tree every year!"
Isabelle continued to exclaim over the baby grand
piano ornament commemorative of the year she got
her real baby grand, and the silver and gold bells
from two of her daughter's weddings and the
wooden pinocchio they brought back from Italy.

After every ornament had been opened and either
selected or discarded, Isabelle applied the bling
which was cheap, brightly colored balls and old
fashioned silver tinsel carefully pinched off in just
the right sized bunch and hung to shimmer and
sparkle whenever the furnace came on and moved
the air in the dining room.

"I think it's the prettiest tree we've ever had!"
Isabelle said for about the 40th year in a row. But
Henry didn't respond. He was snoring on the sofa
so Isabelle put the boxes out on the porch, picked
up the dirty glasses, turned off the lights and woke

Henry up to go upstairs to bed. Just before she fell

asleep, for just a split second she thought about the

news that night. But she was so tired, it didn't keep

her from drifting off.

Chapter 22

Over the next few weeks Isabelle would put fresh greens around the house, tie bows around candle sticks, and scatter a few short strings of lights on mantles and shelves making her home the most lovely place to be late in the afternoon and evening after the sun was down and the spaces of their home took on a warm glow. Isabelle loved her home and never more than at Christmas. Which is why it surprised even her that every day when Henry left for his office in Lakeview, it was still her first choice to get in the truck with him and be dropped off upstairs with her Kindle, her laptop, and her Android not to return until after dark and just in time for the 5:30 News Hour in the evening.

It was particularly at this time when Isabelle was poignantly aware of how important her coffee shop was for her personally. In the past six months the contract negotiations with her florist board of directors had accelerated toward the likely end of her tenure with them. And as she realized that she very likely was about to be retired and contributing nothing toward her and Henry's financial coffers, she at times returned to her feelings of despair about what life was going to be like for her in that event. She felt like she at least knew she would have the coffee shop and that gave her some comfort.

To a great extent the outcome of the negotiations were actually in her control which was causing her to over self-analyze and over self doubt in the decision to be made regarding the renewal of what would likely be very modified position description. Nevertheless, and sure enough, as it turned out, on

November 30, Isabelle made her decision. That day she announced to her florists that she would not entertain any offer they might be considering extending her. She would, in fact, retire.

Isabelle made her announcement in an email to the association president. Opening her laptop at 1:00 she typed out her message. Then, just as she had the day she read the email that resulted in her closing her studio, she just sat and stared at the screen. She read her message and re-read it and sat without doing anything. And then … "send". She clicked it. "Oh, my," she said out loud to herself. "What did I just do?"

That night, though, Isabelle was at peace. After months of indecision and confusion,she was actually feeling liberated and on some level, after months of helplessness, even empowered. She wasn't just owning her decision, she was hoarding it. She didn't tell Henry. She didn't tell her coffee shop friends. She didn't tell her girls. She didn't, in fact, tell anyone. For two whole days Isabelle just went on about her life knowing where it *wasn't* going, not being sure where it *was* going, and keeping to herself the tiny bit of uncertainty she was still harboring. And for the most part she was feeling very okay about it. Then a few days later she got an evening call from a florist and Henry overheard enough to ask what she had been talking about and she told him

"I quit my job," said Isabelle.

There was just the slightest show of surprise by Henry. "When?" he asked.

"A few days ago. And I'm going to keep the coffee shop," she said.

"Well good," Henry said. "That's fine. I think you

should."

And that was about it. Which was a relief and not a surprise to Isabelle. After so many months of agonizing over the decision and talking to Henry, she really wanted it to be just okay. And it was. That's just the way Henry was. It was entirely up to Isabelle. Henry often said he couldn't be married to a stupid person. There were moments like this when Isabelle knew she couldn't be married to a man who thought he owned her. *"How liberating,"* thought Isabelle. And how right it all felt, at least for now.

Henry had just kissed Isabelle on the cheek saying "Early Merry Christmas to you, honey" when Isabelle got a text chime. It was Sammy.

"You guys should come to Chicago and go to the Joffrey Ballet with Joe and me."

"Oh that would be fun!" Isabelle texted back.

Then she turned to Henry and said "Sammy invited us to come to Chicago and go to the ballet with them. You wanna go?"

Waiting for the squirm, the eye rolling, and the hemming and the hawwing, Henry shocked her by replying "Sure!"

"It's a double date!" Isabelle texted back to Sammy. "Get the tickets!" It felt to Isabelle like the perfect way to celebrate the launching of her new life.

So the last weekend before Christmas the two of them were in downtown Chicago walking around the German Christmas market, trying to keep warm, strolling through Lincoln Park, drinking coffee at Magnolia Bakery, browsing through P.O.S.H, admiring the cheeses and meats at Eataly, and of course attending the Nutcracker Ballet! They had dinner with Sammy and Joe at a South African

Restaurant sitting on top of what would have been Camp Douglas in the civil war, which Isabelle only knew about because she was coincidentally reading Irish Lace, a book set in Chicago.

All weekend the snow fell ever so gently at times and the bitter fresh, cold would bit their faces as they walked the sidewalks of Chicago ducking now and then into yet another shop for coffee and a chance to warm up! It was the perfectly magical holiday getaway … until that moment when they were warming themselves in a bakery and Isabelle experienced an unexpected and intense surge of internal panic.

Sitting over their shared coffee feeling a craving for something sweet, Isabelle had been waiting for Henry to ask her if she wanted anything to eat. When he didn't, she had a sudden and acute awareness that she no longer earned money. She was in fact financially dependent. It didn't matter in that moment that she had really always been financially dependent. What mattered was that she didn't have a job or an income. And it didn't feel good.

Counting her scant few dollars she said, "I think I'll get myself a cookie," at which time Henry said, "Here let me give you some money. You don't have much." And then he handed her $40 in the most sincere way. Poor Henry. If only Isabelle could think of him in his best moment, which he deserved. But no, he just enacted what she was despairing over in her mind, lest there be any doubt she was right.

 Isabelle was still feeling the cloud of that moment when later they were talking with Sammy about retirement. After Isabelle joked that she would just wait for Henry at their duplex in Minneapolis if he was going to work seven more years, Henry countered, "Then I'll just charge you rent." Ouch. That was the clincher that put Isabelle in a funk. That statement and the moment she had had to hold her hand out for cookie money, shook Isabelle to her core. Internalizing her painful awareness of her employment status and her financial dependency, Isabelle allowed that cloud to hang over her the rest of the weekend. Coming home to find, in the mail, solicitations from a few of her favorite non-profit organizations, Isabelle was again reminded she no longer had money to donate. Henry was spared Isabelle's fixation about her lack of financial independence because Isabelle got so busy over the next few weeks. But it would likely re-surface eventually.

The girls and their husbands were all coming home for Christmas filling all five bedrooms and making

the quiet house just seem to burst at the seams.
They were both looking forward to opening those
upstairs bedroom doors and furnace vents again and
seeing toys, books, laptops, phones, shoes, coffee
cups, wine glasses, random socks and more
scattered all over the house for the better part of a
week.

 Isabelle had some serious shopping, cooking and
cleaning to do, and it couldn't all be saved for the
last three days before their arrival. So she was too
busy for the rest of the season to give much thought
to her life or politics at all. Once she was 3 days out,
Christmas she got the bedrooms ready. Every bed
got dressed in flannel sheets. Every piece of
furniture got dusted. Every room got a stack of
fresh towels and a white terry cloth bathrobe was
hung on the back of the bedroom doors, one for
each daughter. Once that was done she roasted a

chicken, and baked a ham and pork roast. She

boiled potatoes and eggs, chopped and bagged

onions, celery and carrots, made a couple of pans of

meatballs, and browned a pound of hamburger. She

made sure her bread dough bucket was full and that

she had at least four or five cups of breadcrumbs.

Finally she rolled and cut a batch of homemade egg

noodles.

Isabelle set herself up for spending time with the

kids and not being left behind when everyone went

for a walk.. She wanted to be able to play games

and read stories. So even before everyone came

with their own contributions, the food was literally

stacked to the top of the refrigerator and all her

over-flow was on the front porch. More food was on

its way with the kids. By the time the last car was

unloaded the porch table and shelves would be

covered with dishes, boxes, trays, jars, and meal kits

ready to be brought in and warmed up. There would also be dozens of boxes and tins full of cookies, bars, fudge and candies.

The chaos began as soon as the first car pulled in.

"Henry! Andy's home!" They both ran out to carry in boxes, suitcases, packages, and grandkids who had kicked their shoes off during the 4 hour ride. As May, Sammy, Ivy and their partners arrived everyone went to the driveway to help. Everyone came in talking at once.

"Where are you putting us, Mom?".

"Nonni I'm hungry!"

"Mom, the house looks great!"

"Is there wrapping paper in the basement?"

"Ivy, don't come down!"

"What wants to play Settlers of Catan?"

Someone was playing the piano, the baby was crying, the kitchen table game was getting rowdy, and the coffee grinder was grinding. It never made Isabelle nervous. She soaked it in and savored it. They were filling the house with more memories.

Sammy came down the next morning with her head wrapped in a towel and said, "Okay. I forgot to pack underwear. Schuyler, did you say you're going to Lakeview to lift weights? Cuz if you are you're going to have to stop at the dollar store and pick me out some!"

Eventually everyone had to get back to their own homes and their jobs. Henry and Isabelle had a mountain of sheets and towels to launder and porch full of leftovers to clean up. They found a stray sock, a stuffed animal, someones phone charger that turned out to be theirs, and a book. It was time for life to return to normal again., whatever that was. At any rate, it was time to find out what life was going to be like as a retiree and how her members were doing at the coffee shop. The break from politics had been therapeutic but the next few months were pretty rough most years just because of the cold and the short overcast days. Isabelle was thinking the upstairs coffee shop might need to offer some therapy sessions until everyone got back on track.

PART TWO

Chapter 23

The holidays were over. The election was behind her and Isabelle was facing a clean slate. Retired but recharged she would be figuring out her new normal and what life would be like going forward. She felt liberated but also slightly purposeless. Hoping that her interest in political engagement might lead her to something like an opportunity for resistance, she continued to find the upstairs to be her lifeline and waited patiently for something to find her.

One Friday morning soon after the holidays Isabelle was staring out the window of the upstairs coffee shop at the dirty piles of snow. She looked at the alley that ran behind the shop and beneath the east windows where nothing was moving at all. Streets had been ice covered for a week and temperatures had hovered in the teens and were forecasted to plunge even lower. Henry and Isabelle had weekend plans to go to Ivy's house in Des Moines for the weekend but it wasn't looking good for travel. Looking to the left she could see that the employees of the co-op across the alley were working at their desks. Peering right, she could see all the bank employees cars counting seven of them.

Isabelle made herself a cup of Tetley tea. She enjoyed her tea the way the Brits drank theirs, with a little honey and little cream. Isabelle finally had a quiet solitary opportunity to revisit her now month old decision to retire from her job. And she was pleased with herself that for the most part after all that had happened last year she was at peace.

She had just had her entire family under one roof for three wonderful days. In the ensuing time, since she had suppressed her despair over financial dependency. Soon she would be needed in Minneapolis to help with the grand kids when they welcomed a new sibling. She thought about her life and how perfect it was in many ways. Sometimes it was so perfect it scared her, in fact. Because of her coffee shop, Isabelle had come to really appreciate Lakeview. It felt good having found her community at last. It felt good having just the right balance of everything. So personally, Isabelle was beginning the new year in a good place both emotionally and physically. Not so for some of her members.

Isabelle heard the door close at the bottom of the stairs and pretty soon Harmony walked into the coffee shop. Harmony had sent Isabelle a text message during the holidays that her church had invited her to leave Lakeview so she wasn't surprised when Harmony paused a moment after walking in and said, "I'm going to miss this place."

"How soon will you be leaving?" Isabelle asked.

"I can get keep the house until the end of February," Harmony replied, "but this Sunday is my last one to preach."

"Wow they don't mess around! What about Dyra?"

Harmony had been hosting a high school student for the entire school year. She was a Palestinian and most likely that had been a problem for the church parish. Instead of seeing the hosting of a Palestinian student as the act of Christian outreach and acceptance that it was and an asset that brought diversity to the local high school and community, it was instead viewed as a political statement. And in Lakeview, pastor's don't make political statements except behind closed doors or voting booths. Perhaps what was even worse, though, was

Harmony bringing in a non-Christian. Harmony explained that Dyra and she would move together. It wouldn't be for at least another month before Isabelle would learn that the exchange company had taken Dyra away from her too.

"Where will you go?" Isabelle asked.

"I have no idea right now but I have a few options. I am looking into a call, a chaplain position which would put me outside a structure of any denomination or maybe I'll just go somewhere and knit until something finds me!" Harmony responded.

"I am so sorry, Harmony. We are going to miss you too, you know."

When Harmony joined the upstairs she had asked if it was okay to be a Democrat because she felt she had to be who the church and community wanted her to be when she was outside the coffee shop. Isabelle had of course said it was absolutely okay to be a democrat! But it turned out that Harmony hadn't had the willpower to deny her political convictions and social views on the outside. In such a politically charged atmosphere she just hadn't been able to remain silent on her convictions and her beliefs informed by her understanding of Christian dogma and had in fact begun to feel a responsibility to hold her parishioners to Christian principles.

Unfortunately for her, when her teachings began to be noticeably inconsistent with what her parishioners wanted to believe, her church gradually became less and less enchanted with their pastor. And as is the norm for small rural conservative communities the powers that be determined to get her moved out. The witch hunt was on.

Isabelle had heard rumblings about the dissent and discontent as early as July when Harmony was on a pastoral retreat. A special guest, Lakeview's mayor nonetheless, was upstairs at Isabelle's request one day to have coffee and discuss how to call the local Democratic party to action. At that time Isabelle was looking for help activating the local democrats. In the course of their broader discourse, the mayor, a registered Democrat himself, let slip that the more senior leadership in Harmony's church were holding some "special" meetings while she was away, wink wink. He then blatantly disclosed to Isabelle that they were discussing how to get rid of Harmony and then, knowing you can't put the genie back in the bottle, he asked for Isabelle's confidence. Isabelle could actually keep a secret even though she didn't always do it. But this was one time she kept her mouth shut. It wasn't a rumor Isabelle wished to help spread and she held out hope that their better angels would prevail upon the church leaders and they would become more forgiving and accepting of their flawed and imperfect pastor. It wasn't to be, unfortunately.

So by the end of the year when word was out that Harmony had been given notice, Isabelle was one of the few who was not surprised. One day over coffee Harmony told Isabelle that it was really only a few church leaders who had stigmatized her, though the general congregation had been complicit in their silence.

"Turns out," Harmony said, "I didn't talk about what they wanted to hear. So they were all ready to blame me for the leveraging of the overarching church governance to bring proceedings to terminate my service."

"I really have trouble wrapping my head around it,

Harmony. Did you talk about tolerance and acceptance from the pulpit, by chance?" It was not hard to see that Harmony was angry and not feeling very charitable towards her parishioners.

"You know, I bet I did a time or two,"Harmony said.

'Don't tell me you wore those floral crocks in front of parishioners, did you?

"Guilty."

"Did you sing in public? Like when you were walking down the street, would sing happy songs or anything?"

"Guilty."

"You know how I love you're fringed leather hippie bag, Harmony, so don't take this wrong. But you didn't carry that anyplace but up here, did you?"

"Guilty on all charges, I'm afraid. Did I do

something wrong?"

" Oh, Harmony. Did no one tell you that you are supposed to blend here? You need to have tan skin, a tan car, a tan coat … Oh, I can't believe you weren't told. I am so sorry!"

They were joking because what else could they do. But it was true.

" Harmony, someone should have told you that in Lakeview it takes some kind of nerve to drive an orange car, paint your house purple, talk any kind of politics, or sing in public. If you want to play it safe you talk about the weather.

"Say you're going to a black tie dinner, the best thing you can do is ask someone what they plan to wear. It's the only way to know what is expected of you.

"They'll tell you most people just wear black pants and a nice shirt so if you decide to wear a black velvet dress with spike heels and diamonds, well it is no one's fault but your own, Harmony, when you realize too late that you really don't fit in. You better hope you don't sit by someone who wore her best appliqued sweatshirt, stretch pants and Nike tennis shoes if you want to blend! You did want to blend, don't you, Harmony?" Isabelle asked.

"Uh, not really."

"But don't you see, Harmony, that in a situation like that you could end up sitting by someone in a sweatshirt? That actually happened to me! I was sitting there thinking 'I got this right. *She* didn't. The invitation said black tie.' But then I broke my plastic fork in my chicken breast and cheesy potatoes and I thought 'maybe not. Maybe my sequins and silk are all wrong and I'm off the charts again!

"Ever since then I keep a nice workout ensemble in my closet in case when I go to one of those events I want to just blend," Isabelle said taking a deep breath as she ended her tirade.

"Have you ever worn it?" Harmony asked.

"No. I don't care if they think I'm fancy pants. I kinda like to stand out. I love it when Mabel from south of town is tending bar and while she's filling my wine glass from her box says, 'Well you're sure dressed up!' I just say 'This old thing?! Neh!'"

The thing about Lakeview, Isabelle had always felt, was that it just isn't even really Christian to not fit in. When someone in town dies, you put money in sympathy cards because that is what everyone does. And you go to every visitation no matter how remote the relationship is with the deceased because, well, everyone else goes. And when someone shares on facebook that they need prayers, you rally. You get right there in line and proclaim your intention to pray. And then when there is healing or survival you try to be the first to point out that prayer works.

Isabelle was sick of it all. She was angry seeing what was happening to Harmony. She had seen it over and over in and it was disgusting her. But at her core Isabelle was midwestern nice. She just couldn't pull the trigger on rude. So she resisted being flippant even though many times she had wanted to post on Facebook, "Are you kidding me? Has it not occurred to anyone that there might have been some medical science intervention here?" And rather than challenge the people who posted "prayers" or "praying for you" Isabelle would just post "thinking of you" or "peace." As she had for

30 years, Isabelle just kept it on the down low.

Harmony washed her cup and picked up her bag. "This has been just what I needed, Isabelle."

"Me too," Isabelle said. "I'm just so angry at this town. You don't deserve this."

It was just a week later when there was a post on the upstairs Facebook page by Harmony asking for some help moving things out of her church office across the street into her house. Henry and Isabelle showed up to help for an hour which was good because Isabelle not surprisingly no one from Harmony's church had come to help. She had to wonder if they were all home praying for their church to find a new pastor while she was at their church helping the pastor they had just discarded.

A month later Harmony was again looking for help to move boxes only this time it was on moving day and she was loading a truck. This time Clarys stepped in and for much more than just an hour. Clarys helped Harmony the better part of two days, stored some of her boxes in her own garage, and spent her own money on a room for Harmony who it turned out had no place to go the night the truck was loaded.

And then just like that, one morning in early spring, Harmony drove out of Lakeview leaving behind her coffee cup on a shelf in the upstairs coffee shop. And that is where it continued to sit. Because Harmony was always welcome upstairs. And there would always be a cup for her if she ever had the chance or the inclination to sneak back in in the dark of night!

Chapter 24

Isabelle was opening the coffee shop every day but no one was showing up lately. Maybe it was the cold or post holiday depression but she was worried. She hadn't been seeing much of them since the election. Were they finding any solace at all? Were they venting? And if they were, then where? For those members who had been so engaged in the vibrant late summer get togethers upstairs, political and social discourse was something they needed. The echo chamber of upstairs was better than nothing when their ideology of tolerance, human rights, women's rights, and health care rights was under attack . But where were they? Why hadn't they showed back up? And where were the ones who had never disclosed their political leanings? Were they staying away from upstairs because of the election? Where was Linda. Where was Christy? Why was Carmen not coming in?

Linda had been a regular, almost daily, visitor to upstairs until the election. But she had not returned in weeks. She worked on Mainstreet and most mornings she would come upstairs for her break. Isabelle knew she came to be alone so she would respectfully leave her alone. Linda normally walked in briskly, made herself a cup of tea, and then sat in the green room with the lights off for 15 minutes coloring in the adult coloring book Clarys had brought up one day. Then she would leave. Passing by Isabelle's office walking down the hall she would give her the peace sign and cheerily say, "best 15 minutes of my day!" Isabelle loved those days.

She missed Linda. Isabelle liked Linda because she was a straight shooter. She was no nonsense. She called it like she saw it so if Linda said you looked great, well you knew you looked great. When Linda had first joined upstairs she had shared with Isabelle that she was lonely in Lakeview too. Linda, however, was lonely in a different way. She was spiritually lonely. Deeply faithful, Linda longed for someone to talk to about her faith. Isabelle was the last person in the world who could have been that person but it hadn't seemed to matter in their friendship.

Linda's Catholicism made Isabelle pretty certain they were polar opposites on some women's rights issues. So they just stayed away from political discussions. And that was fine. But had Linda been offended? Would she ever be back?

It was the day before the inauguration. Isabelle was

in the green room reading The New Yorker when she heard a siren. When sirens went off in Lakeview it got your attention. Isabelle turned her head toward the window sill, leaned up and in to see down to the alley, and promptly slid her chin along the dry old wood of the sill driving a sliver right into the bottom of her chin.

"Dammit!" Isabelle had said out loud. "That hurt like hell!"

"Can you come to the coffee shop and help me get a splinter out?" she texted Clarys.

Isabelle had forgotten that Clarys was nursing a sore toe. But there she'ld come, limping down the sidewalk to perform a splinterectomy on Isabelle's face.

"How did you even do this?" Clarys asked as she removed the splinter.

"I heard a siren and I just looked out the window. I get excited when there's a siren in Lakeview. Don't you? I don't want it to be for anything bad but it means something is happening or someone is getting help!" Isabelle said. Clarys gave her her perplexed look as if to say, *"You're a little wack-a-doodle, my friend."* But she remained silent.

"I'll make us some coffee," Isabelle said after she put a band aid on her face.

Clarys sat down and looked at her phone waiting for Isabelle to grind the coffee.

Isabelle poured two cups of coffee and then opened her phone to her twitter app.

"Okay. Here's something that will make you laugh. My brother tweeted this to our president elect. 'Tie a yellow ribbon, bitches!" she read. "You just booked Tony F'n Orlando to perform at the inauguration! A-lister baby!"

"I want to meet him!" Clarys said. The changing the subject she said, "Tell me about this infatuation you have with sirens. That's disturbing on some level."

Isabelle was about to explain when she heard the front door shut and recognized Lar's walk as she heard him come up the steps.

"We're in the green room!" she yelled.

"What happened to you?" Lars asked looking at the band aid on Isabelle's chin.

"I just got excited about the siren and did a face plant into the window sill. It's probably rooted in my urban longings. I don't want crime or anything but I was just telling Clarys how I get excited at the sound of a siren. Do you guys remember that time that older couple went to the grocery store after church and when they came out their car was gone? Oh, wait. That was in Lakeshore. Anyway it turns out they found it Swivel's driveway. He hadn't really intended to steal it so no one was in trouble but they called the cops and everyone stood around waiting to see what was going to happen. It was the most exciting thing that happened in Lakshore all summer that year!"

"Swivel?

"That was just his nickname. People said it was because he could look every which way at once. So they called him Swivel."

"I kind of remember something like that happening in Lakeview once too. Someone reported a missing car and then later it showed up in front of the Stone County Courthouse. No one knew what had happened. It just went missing and then came back mysteriously. The paper reported that they were going to do DNA testing to find the culprit." Clarys laughed.

"Jesus, can you imagine them doing DNA testing in Chicago on a reclaimed car?" Isabelle said. "Unless someone died I doubt they would even look for the car!"

By now Lars had sat down with his tea in the green room. He had been listening to their stories.

"Laugh all you want," Lars said. "At least people here in our little towns have your back! I saw Smiley get out of his car one day in front the bank. The wind was gusting about 60 mph and his money started blowing all over town. I guess he had 15 100 dollar bills! Smiley started yelling and people started running around all over main street picking up money for him. Smiley always said he was glad he was here. If he'd have been in Chicago they would have been trying to get off with a hundred dollar bill."

"Good people," Isabelle said as she began to pick up and get ready to go home.

"Yep," said Lars. "And most of them voted for Trump. I gotta get back to the salt mines. Happy inauguration day tomorrow, you two."

Chapter 25

It was January 20, inauguration day. The day dawned cold and bleak. It actually didn't dawn at all as a thick fog had descended over Lakeview and the sun never rose that morning. The black of night just turned dark gray and sat quietly atop the the bricks and mortar and within the souls of the homes and the people who had the good fortune to open their eyes that morning and live another day. The warmer weather that was finally melting a week of thick ice had brought the fog. As if the dreary sky wasn't enough, it blended right into the ground melting the scant layer of snow that had lightly blanketed the fields. All contrast was gone between sky, field and gray highway. Isabelle commented to Henry that it looked like April, a month she hated for its lack of beauty or warmth. "But at least in April there is hope," she said.

Isabelle had dressed in black that day. She sat silent as she rode to the coffee shop with Henry. Looking out her window at the passing flat, frozen, colorless fields Isabelle thought about the facebook posts she had seen that morning. Her brother had posted an upside down and backwards American flag. Her sister had posted a quote of history where on his inauguration day President Truman had said to Eleanor Roosevelt "Is there anything I could do for you?" to which she had responded, "Is there anything I can do for you? For you are the one who is in trouble now." Isabelle's sister's facebook status was simple and profound. She had written "by end of day today, we will be living in a country led by a president who does not respect me or my daughters." Clarys had changed her profile picture to a black hole. Isabelle had posted nothing.

Since the election of what many Americans thought would be a tyrannical president, passions had not cooled. If anything they had become more heated. Social media was the medium whereby average people could post their opinions and vent or feel heard. Social media could simultaneously rally the forces of good to unite voices, and divide friends and family with inflammatory rhetoric, hate speech and accusations that felt, and often were, personal. Social media was justly taking the hit for encouraging and facilitating "fake news" and "echo chambers", new media buzz words. Immigrants were fearing deportation and women were bracing for loss of their reproductive and health care rights. The country was dividing itself where productive discourse was doomed to fail. No one was listening.

Everyone was yelling. Civility was missing.

The morning of the inauguration Isabelle was lonely. Sitting alone in the green reading room listening to NPR and the swearing in of the Vice President, a lump began to form and then swell in Isabelle's throat listening to the oaths of office. The reality of what she had known for two months was suddenly getting very real. How appropriate that her coffee shop where people had come when shit got too real to process, ended up being the place where Isabelle herself was when the swearing in was broadcast that morning. And how ironic that on inauguration day the coffee shop was empty.

By noon when the nation officially had its new president the day had remained as dark as it started. At four o'clock it still looked just like it had at seven o'clock that morning. By five o'clock that night Isabelle and Henry were heading home in the dark for their wine, the Newshour and some

cabbage soup. The only other thing planned for the

evening was for Isabelle to make her sign for the

Des Moines Women's march the next day.

Isabelle was going to her first protest and she had a

carload of upstairs members riding along. They

were still angry and they were ready to have their

voices heard. So the night of the inauguration with

all preparations in place and a plan to meet and

depart from Isabelle's driveway the next day at

seven thirty, Isabelle slept the sleep of an angry

bitch planning to wake up and rear her ugly head.

At least it made her feel better to think of it that

way!

Chapter 26

"Let's Rally Bitches!"

That was the rallying call from a very excited Isabelle when the upstairs delegation gathered at the state capitol late morning the day after the inauguration to march for human rights. It brought a few smiles and none more so than from Isabelle's two daughters Ivy and May who could never hear their mother swear without laughing out loud.

Isabelle never quite understood what was so funny about her swearing. She hadn't often used such colorful language when she was raising them. Perhaps that was it. She had tried to raise them to have some civility and propriety but one of the memories all four girls loved about growing up was the time Isabelle got mad at Henry for swearing in front of them and Isabelle had told them if they wanted to swear like their dad, they could do all they wanted as long as they were in the barn. They were so little at the time they just giggled. When Isabelle said, "Let's go to the barn and do some cuss'n, girls!" they just couldn't do it. Isabelle had started kicking bales and screaming profanity to no end, egged on by the peals of laughter coming from the little girls. In hindsight she often wondered if she had been teetering on a precipice of insanity. Ever since then Isabelle's use of profanity was amusing if not hilarious to the girls. So she brought it out every now. And the rallying cry for the Women's March seemed the perfect time.

The Women's March had started as an idea with one woman in Hawaii and had unexpectedly mushroomed into a world wide event. While

Isabelle and her group were in Des Moines marching, other women around the world would be marching in other cities making history and breaking records. DC would exceed a half million marchers and have to cancel the actual march. Chicago would be the second largest march in the nation not only exceeding their estimates by more than double but also having to cancel the actual march because of their turnout. Marches in Australia would be as large as 8,000. Other marches would be as small as 30 people in a fishing village in Alaska, but their statement of solidarity with women around the world would go viral on the internet and they would be as celebrated as if they were 30,000. It would turn out to be phenomenal. For Isabelle participating in the march was her validation as a feminist and an activist.

Though it would seem like the whole world was

celebrating the march of solidarity, it would not be without controversy. The Women's March's mission of standing for human rights would be hijacked by other voices seeking expression, such as those who marched to demonstrate their opposition to the new President . There would ultimately be claims that not all women were included because anti-abortionist women's groups who wanted to join would be officially uninvited because of their cause for the restriction of rights. In spite of the controversy and hybridizing of the mission of the march, one thing that would be noticeably missing would be violence. Around the world, there would not be a single reported incidence of violence in the Women's March.

The lack of violence would not yet be known however, as the seven women (which included three daughters of upstairs members) and a single token man in Isabelle's group descended the city bus steps

the morning of the march and gathered to strategize

their day. Isabelle as the organizer of the group

from the start would assume the leadership role that

day for her group of resistors. Having spent her past

two weeks inviting upstairs members to go to the

march, registering herself and Clarys, sharing the

registration link with others, studying the city map

and bus routes, and staying abreast of updates from

the state organizers she knew that it was expected of

her that she should take the lead. Later Isabelle

would remember being in a panic when the

estimated attendance was at 10,000 and she would

be glad she hadn't learned until much later that her

small group had marched with over twice that many

in the end, over ten times the population of

Lakeview. Recalling her panic later, Isabelle would

be glad that she hadn't backed out.

As her small group of eight walked into the middle
of the crowd, heard the speakers begin their
speeches, and joined in the cheering and chanting
Isabelle felt warm tears run down her face. In that
moment she completely forgot her paranoid
intention to stay on the fringes where they could
make a hasty exit to avoid tear gas or a human
stampede. She was no longer fixated on the tips to
remember if one should get arrested at a peace rally.
She and her friends and daughters got swept up in
the energy and the cause that had brought them to
that place in that moment for that purpose.

With tears visibly falling, Isabelle asked someone to
take a picture of her and Clarys. Clarys had been by
her side throughout the campaign, the door
knocking, the phone calling, the debates, and the
election returns. After sharing in the defeat of their
beloved candidate, to be at this rally, marching with

her daughters, Clarys, and thousands of others who believed in the rights of women was almost more than Isabelle could process. It felt so right and so empowering. And she wanted it documented at least with a picture.

There would be many pictures taken at the rally that day. More than a few times Isabelle was asked permission for her picture with the sign she and Henry had made the night before. On one side she had written "Damn You the Patriarchy" and on the other side she had written "4 My Daughters". She had dressed in her orange vest, teal stocking cap, and her vintage Vasque hiking boots she had had for 40 years. Her signature mile long gray braid hung down her back. But most importantly, Isabelle was wearing and sharing the brightest red lipstick she could find. Before leaving her house that morning she had sent a text to Ivy and May saying "let's rally! I will bring the bright red lipstick!" So along with a little money, sunglasses, her ID, a bottle of water and her phone, Isabelle had made sure she packed the lipstick in her Rick Steve's backpack. Which was a good thing. Because no sooner had they entered the Starbucks that morning where they met up with Isabelle to catch the bus to the capitol than Ivy said, "Where's the lipstick, Mom?"

The food truck sliders, the free "Resist" newspapers, the passionate speeches and the vibrant and diverse participants and their signs invigorated and energized the upstairs group. It restored their hope. The dark day of the inauguration had ended and it was feeling like a new day had dawned. Marching alongside the other feminists who had also given up a Saturday, traveled great distances, and weathered the damp cold just to make their voices heard and participate in democracy was affirming for everyone. Three hours later after a quick stop at a coffee shop and some goodbyes, just like that the car was turned back north to take them home. But Isabelle and Clarys were at peace. They might be going back to Lakeview where no one cared or understood what they had done. But they knew. And that was enough for now. It would have to be.

Tomorrow would be another average Sunday. Monday the upstairs would open. The pots would heat. Isabelle would probably light a candle. She would turn on the little electric fireplace and sit down at her computer to check her mail. She might finish an article in The New Yorker, or knit, or read a book. She might see Lars or Clarys or maybe even one of the new members who hadn't been in yet. She would make some coffee late morning and maybe listen to NPR and the media's reports on the Marches across the country. And Isabelle would know that she had been there. She had marched in that March. She had made history. And that would be enough until she found a pathway to some future resistance. Meanwhile she would take care of her coffee peeps.

Chapter 27

Normally in about February every year the mid winter blues would set in in rural Iowans. People in Lakeview would shuffle through town heads down, shoulders hunched against the wind, grunting out their greetings to each other grumbling about the cold, wondering when winter would be over, and generally agreeing that winter was lasting all too long. Some of them would leave for a week or maybe two and visit someplace warm. Others would gut it out and watch movies, drink more beer, pore through seed catalogs, and gain weight eating junk food to stave off depression.

Of course everyone would know who got to travel to a beach in Mexico because they would post on Facebook pictures of themselves wearing swim suits, beach hats, and sipping little drinks with umbrellas in them. They would showcase photos of their ruddy red alcoholic faces and doughy sunburnt bodies saying cheesy things like, "I guess I should have worn sunscreen. Silly me!" The text between the lines was of course, "But don't you see how much fun I'm having and don't you wish you were me?" Isabelle would throw up a little in her mouth and then swear off facebook until she had another political post to share.

Isabelle harbored no envy of her neighbor's winter escapades always happier to have her coffee shop and her own life than to be sharing a beach with viagra infused fat men in speedos. And, she loved winter. She loved her wool sweaters, sock tights, boots, her red and tan blanket scarf, and hot beverages to keep her hands warm. She was amused at people she would see running into stores or restaurants in their flannel pajama pants, hoodies, and flip flops as if it wasn't 13 degrees out. Those were the winter haters. "No wonder people hate winter," she would say. "They simply are too lazy to dress for it."

In fact, Isabelle and Henry both enjoyed winter. They had cross country skis, ice skates and snowshoes and if the snow was timed right so they could enjoy their sport on a weekend they would be out on the trail with their thermos of cocoa, a camera, and maybe some cheese and crackers skiing or snowshoeing to a winter picnic spot. Those were good days.

They had never taken a winter get away other than a year ago when they took the train out to see Henry's brother in Colorado. Isabelle would suggest to Henry that it would be a good idea for them to have a winter getaway or a long weekend even it it was just to northern Minnesota where she would sip polar bear coffee and sit in a hot tub surrounded by snow. Even if it wasn't warm, she would assert, it would be a change of scenery and it would be good for them to break up the winter that way. But despite her travel aspirations, as she neared the one year anniversary of the coffee shop, it wasn't to be. Instead, February found her in her daughter Andy's house in Minnesota waiting for the arrival of her fourth grandchild. Henry was left behind to bach it.

Isabelle and Andy had made the plan for Isabelle's visit based on an expected early arrival of a fourth baby and since she had all kinds of time now, she went over a week ahead of the due date. As it turned out Andy's baby was eight days late, which meant that with waiting for the baby and then helping with the baby, Isabelle was gone from home and the coffee shop an entire month.

Isabelle later referred to that month as her sabbatical, after Henry explained that sabbaticals are intended for introspection and self improvement. Other than missing Henry she was doing her introspecting and self-improving in urban paradise. She had plenty of alone time while the kids were in school to do some neighborhood hiking, have lunch with a few friends, shop in little boutiques for the end of winter sales, and sit in coffee shops and write or read The New York Times on her laptop. Every evening she and Henry would talk by phone or skype. Isabelle would give animated accounts of how she had spent her day and how much she loved Minneapolis. Henry would update her on his latest project which was refinishing a floor in their house. They would often end in a stalemate discussion of their dreams for retirement and then both of them would have sleepless nights anguishing over how to amicably navigate the next chapter of their long marriage.

During her month Isabelle pledged to herself that she was going to make some changes when she got home. She still had not found anything else to engage her other than her coffee shop and its members. For one, she was going to start sewing again. Henry would like it if she was in the basement sewing in the evening while he worked in his shop. And she thought she might take piano lessons again. She loved playing but she rarely did.

Before her "granny sabbatical" she had been getting a little depressed about upstairs and had been feeling like she was a laughing stock and her shop was a failure. It seemed like no one was interested anymore and maybe she should start spending more time at home where she could cook and have neighbors in for coffee like the old days, instead of hanging out upstairs so much. While Isabelle was spending her time away thinking about how to enjoy the next decades with Henry, Henry was doing the same thing at home. Isabelle later likened Henry's time at home, while she was gone, to a staycation by referring to it as Henry's staybbatical.

Sabbaticals turned out to be good for them both. When they re-united for a romantic weekend at their cabin with long walks, deep discussions, afternoon naps topped off with coffee followed later by evening wine they were ready to face their future. And arriving home at the end of their weekend at the cabin after an entire month away, Isabelle was happy to find herself back upstairs the following Monday morning making coffee and catching up with her friends.

It was already the first of March and spring was feeling close. Daylight savings time and cold press were back and the members seemed to be coming back too. The month had been long for the upstairs as members who came to have coffee with Isabelle had missed her and now learning she was back, members, like her friend Christy, were finding time to stop in again. Isabelle was encouraged again after her late January funk. She was excited to have five new members in the upstairs co-op and she had some AIRBNB bookings on the calendar and that always lifted her spirits. Isabelle was back to her old eternally optimistic self.

Chapter 28

Isabelle was washing dishes at the coffee shop when she got a text from Christy one warm spring morning. Christy had been away too long and Isabelle wasn't sure why so seeing the message that she would come up for coffee if Isabelle was there, pleased Isabelle.

Christy and Isabelle had been acquaintances for years but there had been little opportunity for their friendship to develop. Isabelle was at least 20 years older than Christy and they were in different stages of their lives. They had first crossed paths several years ago in the press box overlooking the Lakeview football field when Isabelle was spotting for Henry and , Christy was sound checking for a student to sing the national anthem.

DID ANYONE PROOFREAD THIS BOOK?

"We should have coffee sometime," Christy had said one night while they were standing and waiting for the clock to wind down.

That always seemed kind of strange to Isabelle. She couldn't imagine why Christy would want to have coffee with her or what she saw that they had in common. Isabelle thought it might be due to having raised a family and Christy was looking for support, as she too had four children and a husband who was barely home. Isabelle would later realize what Christy obviously knew, that just being liberal women in a rural conservative community navigating life was enough basis for a friendship. Christy had needed a mentor and she had spotted Isabelle.

Years passed and they never had coffee together. Then one day, acting on a new year resolution to be more social, Isabelle called her.

"Christy, hi. It's Isabelle Potts. Got a minute?" Isabelle asked over the phone.

"Sure. How are you?"

"Well I'm fine and I am in the mood cooking. I wondered if I could make supper for your family Sunday night. I remember what it's like to have a family to cook for and thought you might appreciate a night off."

"Oh, how nice! I would love to but Kelvin is on the road and he won't be until Monday night. Shoot! That's so nice of you!"

"No worries. I knew it was a long shot but thought I would ask. We'll try another time," Isabelle hung up the phone. *"That was awkward,"* she thought.

After multiple failed attempts to find a time that worked for everyone Isabelle gave up with shattered confidence. Months later she tried one last time and they they were free to come. Isabelle remembered it as a great evening. Everyone seemed to enjoy it but it proved to be a one time date. It was just too hard to catch Christy's family on a free night.

And then until the coffee shop, a few years later … nothing more developed in their friendship. It even got weird to run into Christy in the grocery store because they just didn't have any social over-lap other than what Isabelle had forced. Upstairs changed that dynamic. It was a kind of neutral zone making it different than inviting Christy and her family into the intimacy of their home. So when upstairs opened, Christy got invited to join and that was when their friendship really began.

Christy had a beautiful, albeit feisty, soul. She had a bounty of naturally curly dark auburn hair. She made no apologies or excuses for her size 12 body exuding confidence in her manner and sporting fashion in her personality. She wore wild leggings, stylish boots, and shared a healthy amount of cleavage. She liked her coffee often and she liked it strong so upstairs was her happy place.

It would be Christy who would be the member coming up to vent about the mansplaining and manterrupting she was subjected to in her local teachers union. Christy would be the member to show up in a rage about the other women teachers who in the teacher's lounge would say they don't get what the resistance is all about. She was the resident feminist at the public school and as Isabelle was to learn, in her home where the "man of the house" had voted for Trump.

Isabelle read the text message. "Are you upstairs?"

"Yes," Isabelle texted back.

A few minutes later Isabelle heard the door shut

downstairs and then Christy's beautiful voice

singing Carole King's 1971 Tapestry album hit You

Make Me Feel Like a Natural Woman.

"Whoa girl! Kelvin must have got home last night!"

Isabelle said,

"Aren't you just the smart ass this morning! As a

matter of fact he did."

"Well you can sign any song you want up here. I

love it. I would give my right arm to have your

voice. I can't sing AT ALL."

"Anybody can sing," Christy said.

"How is Kelvy, by the way? You should bring him

up for coffee sometime."

"He's fine but exhausted. He's been on the road all

week and needs some sleep.And I would NEVER

bring Kelvin up here for coffee. This liberal bastion is not his cup of tea or coffee."

"I know. I was mostly kidding. But how do you do it, Christy? How do you navigate political conversations with a husband who has such different views?" Isabelle asked.

"Mostly you just don't talk about it. We're all more than just our politics, right? But I'll say this … this year has been harder than ever. I mean this year feels just raw at times. I'm not over the election and it's what, March? I'm a feminist. I'm raising two daughters I want to to be feminists. And their daddy voted for Trump."

"The man who gropes women and brags about it." Isabelle said.

"Exactly! I was in the car with Kelvin the other day and we were talking and I finally turned to him and said 'Who even *are* you?' and he said to me 'who even are *you?*'

"We know when it's time to just shut up. But honestly, Isabelle, I don't think Kelvin is all that in love with Trump. He just hates government regulation. He hates that the government is so involved in our daily lives so he'll vote party line no matter what."

"Clearly!" Isabelle said. "For the record, though, I want a woman president in the worst way but a poor female candidate wouldn't get my vote. I don't know what I would have done if the best my party had was a Palin or Trump. But I know what I wouldn't have done. Not to change the subject but did you know there are two residences in Lakeview flying Confederate Flags?"

"Not surprised at all. We have a lot of hate in this

town," said Christy

"Did I tell you about Henry's client with the dog names Niggs?"

"WHAT?!"

" Yea. He had an emergency call Saturday night for an injured dog. I rode along to the clinic. This big guy gets out of his truck. He's big. He's as tall as Kevin and he's carrying his dog and I had him pegged right away. Made me a little nervous actually. He was kind of scary. Henry had to hospitalize the dog for the weekend. I guess the dude said he had left in a hurry and forgot his wallet but wondered if Henry wanted his gun that he keeps under the front seat of his pick up until he could get back in Monday."

"What did Henry do?"

"He told the guy he thought he could trust him. Henry said they guy was a soft heart. I guess he got a little tremor in his voice when he talked about his dog, "said Isabelle.

"Oh man. Go figure."

"Exactly. I can't even wrap my head around it," Isabelle said as Christy stood up and went to the kitchen to wash her mug.

"Hey, I gotta go. It's dance night. You gonna be here on Friday?"

"Not sure," Isabelle said. "But shoot be a text. Shop will be open even if I'm not."

"I know. I come to see you. I'll check in with you"

"Alrighty! Drive safely tonight," Isabelle said as she started picking up the coffee shop to head home herself. Isabelle washed the few dishes, put away

the ones that had been sitting in the drainer to dry,
and started soaking a pot of ground beans for
tomorrow's cold press. She was thinking about
Christy and how she was pretty sure she was her
political and social justice ally, maybe even her
kindred spirit. But a fellow resistor … probably not.
And she wouldn't ask her to be when she heard
Christy walk back into the coffee shop.

"I can't take time to tell you anymore but did you
hear about the Podunk Resistance?" Christy asked.

"No, what's that?"

"It's a group of about 5-6 people that go to a
podunk town every week and peacefully protest for
15 minutes and then they go someplace where they
serve wine and eat together. Thought you might be
interested," Christy said as she left once again.

Isabelle gathered her things and headed downstairs

to meet Henry for her ride home. But she stored

away that tidbit of information intending to find out

more.

Chapter 29

Thinking about the five new members in the

upstairs coffee co-op, Isabelle was encouraged

enough to think about phase two of the upstairs

coffee shop. Her January discouragement had

prompted her to think about ways to revitalize it.

Her political interests seemed to have no outlet for

expression anymore, other than the coffee shop

gatherings. With her job being over she was having

second thoughts about keeping her office space and

subsidizing the coffee shop at the level she had been

when she was working.

One of her ideas was to move it to the upstairs of

the fitness gym. She saw the move as an

opportunity to serve a broader community and expand the menu to protein shakes as long as she could do it without compromising the privacy vibe and obscurity her members expected her to protect . The young entrepreneurial owner of the gym happened to be a coffee shop member and was more than interested in the idea. So the two of them started talking about how to collaborate and what the business model would be if they partnered.

Isabelle envisioned outdoor rooftop seating, a better kitchen, cheaper rent, and the biggest bonus … a room with a fireplace. Her enthusiasm turned out to be infectious and several members and Henry were on board. So as temperatures plummeted to the single digits in mid-march, which seems to happen every year just before the onset of spring, Isabelle was back in full form strategizing and even beginning to execute phase two for an injection of vibrancy she felt might be lacking.

Vibrancy was always what Isabelle was hoping to bring to Lakeview by having a coffee shop. She knew she couldn't invigorate the entire town with it but she thought she could at least create an oasis of it for the upstairs members. Recognizing that youth and vibrancy go together, Isabelle had exerted real effort in getting young members to join. She would almost give them free coffee to get them to come upstairs and check it out. And her strategy worked. Young members came and brought just what Isabelle was looking for but she would learn that they were also looking for something.

Several of the young members Isabelle would learn, were looking for mentoring on how to deal with their feelings of isolation living in Lakeview. They were bright young adults in every single case and in many cases they were back in Lakeview after having lived in Chicago, Iowa City, or Des Moines. Several of them were well travelled and all of them were aware of what they were missing and what they would never have if they stayed. They were afraid of never getting out and when the national spotlight put Lakeview and their part of the state in the news because of racial comments made by Steve King, Isabelle knew that what they needed to hear from her was not just understanding but hope for a pathway forward if they never escaped Lakeview. So even though she wanted to tell them to get out as fast as they could, she would mostly listen and then share her own story of how she had been able to make living in Stone County and King country work for her.

A young female member was getting her coffee one day when she said, "I don't know how much more of this place I can take. I hate it here."

"Let me tell you the story of a conversation I had with my niece, Bella, one day when she came to visit me in Lakeshore," Isabelle said.

"Bella was visiting from Kansas City. She is privileged, white and sheltered and she is surrounded by urban amenities and opportunities. She was about 15 years old at the time, and she was smart and sophisticated beyond her years. Anyway, we were on a walk in Lakeshore when she had made an unflattering comment about Lakeshore that struck a nerve," Isabelle said.

"You felt defensive of Lakeshore?!"

"Well I don't think of it that way. I'll tell you what I told her. I like to think of Lakeshore as real. It's a town where real people are living real lives plodding along the best way they know how. When I read, I like to read novels set in far away places.

The ones I find most interesting are the ones set in little European villages, hamlets and towns sprinkled around the rural areas of the countries. Those are the places where the characters that color the community and make it what it is come to life."

"I actually like the same kind of book," the young member responded.

"And when I go to Europe, I want to visit those places. I don't want to go to the cities where the tourists go to visit the museums and cathedrals. I want to visit the little villages where I can see a slice of the real authentic lives of the culture I'm visiting. I want to read about those towns and get a peek inside the homes and lives of the characters that live there.

"As depressing as it is you have to understand that the people in Lakeshore may be here because they have no place else to go. Many of them are fully aware of what they are not capable of, what they will never have, and that they are living on the fringes of a society they don't get to fully participate in," Isabelle said.

" But these are resilient people. They know this might be as a good as it will ever get and they make it work. And I like to think that right here in rural Iowa where we live we are experiencing something that can only be understood by living here. We *are living* in that little European village I'm talking about. We have a front row seat.

"Where we live, you and I know almost everyone in town. I have received phone calls from someone who has a wrong number. I have known who they are by the sound of their voice and even been able to tell them the correct phone number of the person they meant to call." Isabelle wasn't done.

"When we go to the grocery store I have to walk past the local pedophile sitting on the bags of water softener salt. Living here we may not have ethnic or cultural diversity but what we do have is the socioeconomic diversity of sitting by the banker or the high school dropout living off disability and mowing people's lawns for a living when we go to a fundraiser pancake supper." "Kids here don't go to private schools or live in "better" neighborhoods like my niece did. Everyone knows which kids don't have socks to wear in the winter. They know whose mom is on meth and whose dad is in jail. They sit by them in school. They play on the same team with them in basketball." Her young member remained silent listening to Isabelle.

"When Andy was in school, we would pick up one of those kids to make sure she got to games. Andy would go in her unlocked house to get her out of bed and out to the car so we got her to the game. People in town knew which kids probably hadn't had supper when they were hanging out at the kids rec concession stand on summer nights with no money, and most anyone there would buy them a hotdog and they didn't care what color they were or that their family was on public assistance. When little girls nine years old were coming to church by themselves it was a safe bet they were getting away from something at home.

"There is a lot I don't like about living here and I hope I don't live here forever, but it isn't lost on me entirely the richness that has been a part of my life for having lived here. And that the people I just described to you who fill in the missing pieces for the disenfranchised are the same people that voted for Trump and against entitlements for themselves and their neighbors. I cannot explain that to you,

But I can tell you it isn't the whole picture."

The young woman was quiet as she finished her
coffee.

"It's just something to think about," Isabelle said.
"We all need to be better at blooming where we are
planted and I hope don't take as long to figure that
out as I did."

Chapter 30

A day upstairs spent with a young member was a good day for Isabelle. But it could also be an exhausting day because she felt such responsibility for them. Days with her friends Carmen and Clarys were normally much more relaxing. But not always.

Both Carmen and Clarys had been members in the upstairs since its inception a year ago. So what they thought about an idea or an issue was important to Isabelle. Even though she was independent and could be stubborn, she knew she needed their support if she were to move the upstairs to above the fitness center. Clarys seemed to be all for it, Carmen on the other hand, was dragging her feet on the idea.

To be fair, Carmen was struggling with having another birthday which Isabelle only found out about one day when she came for coffee and shared how much she had been crying lately. Clarys happened to be absent at the time, helping a struggling friend up at the lakes, so Isabelle was alone when Carmen arrived upstairs one morning.

The two women hadn't had coffee together in months so to meet at the table over french pressed house blend was a treat. Java therapy was all any of them ever really needed. This day Carmen was especially missing her family in Spain. Her birthday was five days away and she was dreading it. Isabelle listened mostly and sipped her coffee. It really was her only to choice to listen; Carmen was a talker and didn't stop very often for others to talk. Sometimes even when they did, she interrupted them. It wasn't that she meant to be rude. She was just passionate in a Latin sort of way. It could both infuriate and endear Isabelle to her.

So that morning, though Isabelle thought she might be able to help Carmen by arming her with some self help tools, she knew she had to catch her when she had her attention. She waited until there was a lull when Carmen wasn't talking ... and then Isabelle seized her chance.

"Have you ever heard of mindfulness, Carmen?" Isabelle asked.

"No."

"Well mindfulness is about being mindful of the moment you are in. Mindfulness is saying to yourself when you are consumed with regret or paralyzed by fear and worry, that if you don't stop it you will miss this moment in which you find yourself right now. You see, Carmen, we can't fix what is already past. And we can't predict what will happen tomorrow. And if we spend all of our time in guilt or regret, or worrying about the future, we miss the moment. And it will never come around again. Once it's gone, well ... it is gone forever. So try to do that when you find yourself feeling guilty or worrying. Just tell yourself to stop it, give yourself a little forgiveness, and try to enjoy the moment. You have been a wonderful mom, Carmen. You're kids are all fine and they are independent now so you should be enjoying this time with your husband and seizing the moment. Carpe Diem, Carmen!"

Isabelle stopped and waited to see if anything she said had penetrated Carmen's stubborn demeanor. Even though she couldn't tell for sure, it was a good sign that she had been able to deliver her entire message without interruption. It was possible she thought, that while dabbing at her tear-filled eyes, Carmen had been listening. Carmen soon stood up to leave and gave Isabelle a tight hug and said "I have to get to work but thanks friend. I needed this." And then Carmen headed down the long hallway and Isabelle picked up the press and went to the kitchen to wash some dishes and bake a coffee cake for the afternoon. "This is why I do this", Isabelle thought. "This is why I have a coffee shop. This town needs this. My friends need this." And though she may never know if Carmen would practice mindfulness, she had no doubt she had helped her at least a little bit that morning.

Helping people was something that helped Isabelle, really. Indeed it was a great part of why she hosted guests in her airbnb. Sure, there were selfish reasons like the extra money and the cultural exposure but nothing really gave her more enjoyment than taking in a weary traveler making their day just a little better. Which is just what she did later that same day.

Isabelle was visiting with another one of her new young co-op members when her phone rang in mid-afternoon and the display said Kansas, where her expected guest was from. Answering her phone she learned that the poor guy was lost in Lakeview and running late to his business appointments. He had spent an hour in a snow bank earlier that morning having slid off the icy roads and with his GPS failing out in the country where he couldn't pick up a signal. He had barely been able to identify to AAA where he was. In a suit and dress shoes, with Iowa temps in the teens he was understandably not warming to Iowa where he was going to be spending the the next three weeks.

"Head north on Main Street toward the courthouse,"

Isabelle had said. "When you see the gnome on the toy factory, park your car. It will be on your right. You will see a glass door ..." Isabelle hung up the phone after completing her instructions. And then, smiling, she continued to talk out loud to herself, "Look both ways before you open the door. If no one sees you, quickly open the door, duck in, and head up the stairs. You will see the glow of a room in front of you at the end of the hall. It is the reflection off a gold painted wall. Continue straight. Go in that room. I will be there. Don't tell anyone where you have been or that you had coffee."

Moments later her guest arrived and Isabelle served him an Americana while hearing about his no good terrible very bad day. An hour later they were on their way to Isabelle's and Henry's house where she showed him to his room leaving a bottle of water and two home baked chocolate chip cookies on his dresser.

Later when she and Henry were sharing wine and
their warm fire with their guest who had made it
into jeans, soft shoes, and a sweater, they enjoyed
stories about his travels to Tel Aviv, Paris, and
Chile. "Win, win" thought Isabelle as she drifted off
to sleep at the end of her day. Maybe even win, win,
win …

Chapter 31

March 31, Isabelle walked into her coffee shop with no plans for her day. She set out some freshly baked oatmeal cookies, filtered the pour over brew, set the kettles to heat. She plugged her mp3 player into her speakers and selected the jazz playlist. Stalling before she opened her computer to reply to a facebook message that was conflicting her, she brushed the shelves clean, vacuumed the floors and sorted through the NYT magazines that she let pile up deciding what to save and what to purge. Finally she opened her laptop.

Isabelle's daughter Andy had posted a status of her frustration with male colleagues whose workplace rules, established because of their jealous wives, disallowed them to meet privately or have lunch with female colleagues. She shared that such rules between them and their wives was making it difficult for professional women to get mentored. Andy had vented her frustration in working with such men. Henry had responded "I can't wait to hear what your mother has to say about this".

Sitting with her open laptop thinking about what to say Isabelle finally typed, "Men need to behave professionally and not bring their marital rules into the workplace. They should not hold their colleagues responsible for dealing with jealous wives."

The response had not been an easy one for Isabelle. She had kept it brief but there was so much more she had wanted to say. She was able to articulate it later when she and Clarys and Carmen were having coffee.

"What I also wanted to say but didn't" she told them, "was 'Don't make those wives out to be the villains. Their jealousy is very real. There is a good chance that many of those wives, due to lacking something … maybe self confidence, maybe opportunity, maybe money, or maybe even just encouragement … have found themselves, now too late, stuck in a trajectory that is no longer reversible. They may have kids. They may be living in a place where there are no jobs, and no opportunity to get an education. They are likely financially dependent. And they are very aware that they are being left behind. Many of them know they have undersold themselves. And they are painfully aware that now it's too late. They face that every day their husbands walk out the door to head to their jobs. On the back side of that closed door they are standing knowing there are no open doors for them to walk through. I've been that wife!" Isabelle said. "25 – 30 years ago I didn't have time to read a daily paper. I had four kids. I was canning. I was sewing. I was having babies. I wasn't glamorous. I may have nagged. I probably looked like a hag. And I was keenly aware that every damn day, my husband was going to a workplace where the female employees looked nice, did everything he asked them to do, and were intellectually engaging! Was I jealous? You bet I was. But it was mine to deal with, not Henry's and certainly not Henry's employees. And I did deal with it. Then 20 years ago I got lucky. I got a chance to jump into what turned out to be a 19 year career that restored my faith in myself a little. So it got better for me but it doesn't for everyone. So I get how those wives are feeling. And I get how my daughter is frustrated. But don't make that wife out to be the villain. She isn't. Her spouse needs to man up and do his job, but leave the wife out of this. There may come a day when one of my daughters berates herself for something in her past. Maybe it will be for following a career path instead of staying home with her kids. I don't know. I hope not. But whatever it is, I don't want women who made a different choice vilifying her for her choice. We only get to live one life. That's it! We all have choices to make and we do our best and we need to support each other. That's all."

Isabelle took a deep breath and sat silently. She was exhausted. Clarys looked at her slack jawed. Carmen chimed in with her own self deprecating comments. After some affirmations of their worth to each other and assurances that they had all always been enough, the three women parted for the weekend. Clarys had friends to visit at the lake,

Carmen had family coming for the church auction and Isabelle was off to Des Moines for a delayed farewell luncheon in her honor by the 16 past presidents of the floral association she had managed. Isabelle drove home encouraged that the days were getting noticeably longer.

Chapter 32

That night Isabelle was still preoccupied with her rant. She tossed and turned all night worried she wasn't getting enough sleep for her drive the next day. She left feeling reflective the next morning spending two hours thinking about all that had happened in her life and in the last year as she drove to Des Moines.

She was 63 years old and she had had a good life. She had been married to the same man for 42 years and they were still wholly and passionately in love with each other. They were finally starting to talk about what retirement was going to look like for them and it was looking like it would exceed her wildest dreams if all worked out. Isabelles daughters were all happy, educated, and strong feminists on success tracks. She had no regrets and no reason to complain. She knew that, objectively.

But in spite of all that, last year had been tough. Isabelle had opened the coffee shop before she knew what political and personal turmoil she was going to be facing in the next months. It was a good thing she had opened upstairs because it had turned out in many ways to be her lifeline throughout the year. She had spent a good part of the year being unkind to herself, self doubting, second guessing, feeling ashamed and even embarrassed at times. She had felt useless and purposeless and hadn't always been able to see her path forward. Her friends and the coffee shop had been a place to find solace and understanding. She had felt good about the coffee shop and what it had meant to the members. It had been a happy place for her. She felt good about what she meant to the members. She had mentored them and supported them and had given them a community some of them didn't even know they had needed.

But during the months of negotiations and reviews surrounding her job with the florists she had been hard on herself. She had blamed herself for not managing the association better. She felt like under her watch they were going down and she had scrutinized her 19 years of management trying to figure out where she had gone wrong and how she had let them get to this point. Later in the year when the election was final and coffee shop women were coalescing around their shared experiences of discrimination in the workplace, Isabelle had felt shame. She felt she had undersold herself for not having sought more education and a profession and she felt undeserving of speaking to the issues of the sisterhood that she had not experienced herself because while they had been on the front lines, she had been in the kitchen canning and in the living room rocking her babies. She felt unworthy of the nasty woman movement. She felt unworthy of so much.

Isabelle had looked at her life critically and unkindly and without forgiveness. Yet all the time she had never failed to recognize what her contribution had been to her family. She knew Henry was proud of her. She knew she had won the lottery when it came to having daughters she could be proud of and she allowed herself to take some credit for how they had developed into the women they had become. So even while she self-recriminated, she didn't regret. She only wished she had done more. Accomplished more. Demonstrated more. Sought more. Aspired to more.

Isabelle arrived at her luncheon feeling some

nervousness about being the guest of honor but eager to see some of her favorite florists. She had needed closure, having departed her position in the shadow of a tyrannical association president who had reprimanded her for even a farewell message to the sitting council members. Today was to be that closure. And it turned out to be all that more.

Isabelle was floored when she saw that eight of the 16 past presidents who had been invited had come. They had driven from as far as both the east and west borders of the state and as far north as the twin cities. Several of them had brought their spouses and a few of them had brought small gifts.

Over the next two hours they shared hugs and stories and took lots of pictures. And then they handed Isabelle a package. Inside it was a cashier's check for $1600. Isabelle gasped, her eyes filled with tears, she looked up at the table full of people who had valued and loved her for the part she had played in their life and she saw many of them wiping their own tears. She was speechless but she managed to utter a humble thank you as she picked up from the package a ribboned bundle of letters. "Each of us has written you a letter, Isabelle", someone said. "Thank you," Isabelle whispered.

Isabelle drove home later feeling more spiritually lifted and inwardly peaceful than she had in a very long time. She had not known how much she had needed this closure. She was beginning to believe that whatever the future, she would be okay and she would adapt. Isabelle had been on a roller coaster of emotions over the last year struggling with her place in the grand scheme of things but she knew that she had always been resourceful and she had to believe that would see her through as it always had. In fact, it was time to check out the Podunk Resistance. She was ready.

The year had left her stronger and wiser and, though not necessarily more empowered, it had not left her any less empowered either. She was entering her next life phase resolved to be more accepting of things she could not change. Though Henry and she had talked of retirement plans, she knew in her heart of hearts that as much as Henry loved her, her dream of living in a city before she died may not ever come to fruition. The dream of urban walks, the ready access to bike trails, coffee shops, book stores, the free park concerts, and the bug free outdoor sidewalk bistros needed to be put aside.

Their marriage had mostly been a 50/50 partnership that Isabelle knew she had claimed against all odds and that few women her age could claim. But she also knew she may never escape Stone County and that in the end her husband would be the one to decide what and when they pulled the trigger on a major life change. And she wasn't so sure she didn't prefer it that way. She was done with her pity party and pledged to herself that from now on it wasn't going to be all about her. She was committed to blooming where she was planted, appreciating what she had, savoring the moments and tapping into her resourcefulness again.

When the girls had all been in school and she could see that Henry needed help from her to bring in revenue, recognizing the limited choices for a an educated woman in Stone County, Isabelle had looked outside Stone County diving into state association management headfirst. When the last daughter had gone to college and Isabelle had wondered *"Now what?"* she had launched her photography business. When that had finally run its course, Isabelle opened her upstairs coffee shop.When she had yearned for more travel and cultural exposure, lacking funding and time she had remembered the Turkish proverb about Muhammad going to the mountain and she had listed on AIRBNB and opened her home to strangers. Now that her 19 year career in association management had come to an end, Isabelle needed once again to dig deep inside herself figure it out. She was nothing if not resilient and resourceful and there would be something for her to do that was purposeful and productive. Participation in the Podunk Resistance was calling her. Perhaps that would be it.

 Later that night she sat on the sofa reading through the letters. They had given her the affirmation that had been missing; that she hadn't given to herself. Her family had always affirmed her. Her friends had often told her she was enough. But she had always felt lacking in spite of that. She read through the comments ...

- "Thank you for all you taught me over the years. Thank you for showing me grace."

- "You taught me to listen. You taught me to stay the course. You had my back. Thank you."

- "When I think of my year as president, it is your presence that comes to mind. You were always present at everything making sure things ran and every detail was addressed. Thank you."

- "Thank you for speaking up when we needed to hear the hard lesson. Thank you for making us do the right thing even when it might not have been the popular thing."

They went on and on. Isabelle was deeply touched by their kind words. She folded up the letters and tying the string around them she laid them on the china cabinet. She would put them away somewhere tomorrow. She would keep them in a shoe box or a binder to be found and read again or perhaps to be discovered by a daughter or a grandchild who would read them and see her in a different light. It was enough for now that they saw her as their mother or grandmother, but someday Isabelle wanted them to know she had been more. She had mattered in other ways. Nothing in her world mattered more than them, but there had been more in her world and she wanted them to know that. It didn't have to be today. But someday.

Isabelle folded the afghan and laid it on the back of the sofa. She plugged her phone in to charge overnight. She turned the light off on the hutch and walked through the kitchen putting a few dishes in the dishwasher so when she came down in the morning the kitchen would already be picked up.

"I'm heading up," she said to Henry as she stepped on the landing to go upstairs.

"I'll be up in a minute," Henry said.

Isabelle put on her blue plaid night shirt and put a long braid in her hair. Then she brushed her teeth and slipped into the flannel sheets. As she drifted off to sleep thinking about the $1600 dollars she had been gifted and remembering all the times she and Carmen and Clarys had talked about travelling together, she had one last thought of the day ...

- *"Tomorrow I am going to tell Carmen and Clarys that we are going to Spain."*

- ***The End -***

RECIPES

BNB GUEST BREAD IN DUTCH OVEN

Mix together by hand:

3 cups flour

¼ tsp yeast

1 ¼ tsp salt

1 ½ c. water

Let sit in bowl for 15-20 hours. Preheat dutch oven to 500 degrees.

Remove bread from bowl and hand form into a mound. Place it in the hot dutch oven, cover and bake for 30 minutes. Remove the cover and bake 5-10 minutes longer to brown.

SALAD IN A JAR

Place dressing of choice in bottom of pint jar

Layer in bacon bits, dried cranberries, walnuts, olives, hard boiled egg, feta cheese, etc.

Fill balance of jar with cut up lettuce.

Cap and keep upright in fridge until ready to serve. Then turn over on plate.

SWEET CREAM COLD PRESS

Using a pint jar with 3-5 ice cubes add the
following:

5 ounces cold press

3 ounces table cream or half and half

1-2 teaspoons simple syrup

Stir and enjoy

CABBAGE SOUP

Boil the following ingredients in 6 cups of water or
chicken broth

6 carrots

6 stalks celery

1 quart of whole tomatoes cut up

½ onion chopped fine

1 ½ pounds browned ground beef

salt and pepper to taste

BUTTERNUT SQUASH RAVIOLI

For Filling

Cut and seed medium sized butternut squash

Place on cookie sheet and roast in 350 degree oven until blistered and caramelized

Scoop out squash and season with salt and pepper to fill pasta squares

For Pasta

1 whole egg and egg whites from 3 eggs

1 Tbsp Water

2 cups flour

Mix all ingredients together and knead to homogenize. Roll out or run through pasta machine to make a thin sheet. Cut into 3x3 squares to form pocket for filling. Place a teaspoon of filling in center of square. Fold diagonally and seal to make triangle shaped raviolis

CRACKED MARINATED OLIVES

1 pound Sicilian or large green olives, drained

4 cloves garlic, peeled

1 lemon cut in wedges

2 tsp coriander seed

4 sprigs fresh thyme

4 feathery stalks fennel

1 or 2 small red jalapeno peppers

Lightly mash olives on a cutting board using a rolling pin. Using the flat side of chef's knife, smash garlic. Using a mortar and pestle crack the coriander seeds. Divide all ingredients equally between 8 pint jars. Fill jars to rim with Spanish Extra virgin olive oil to cover. Place lid and leave at room temperature for 24 hours. Wait 2 weeks to allow marinade to permeate the olives.